TO:

Wyoming friend,
Pat —

May your many
lives slow down
enough for you
to enjoy the
wonderful sound
of Christmastime.

Jerry
Sullivan
1995

The Sound Of Christmastime

& Other Yuletide Yarns

Gerald D. Sullivan

Library of Congress Number 92-80174

ISBN 1-56044-143-7

Manufactured in the United States of America

Published by SHAMROCK IN THE SKY BOOKS, 1403 S. Bozeman Avenue, Bozeman, Montana 59715, in cooperation with SkyHouse Publishers, an imprint of Falcon Press Publishing Co., Inc., Helena, Montana

Design, typesetting, and other prepress work by Falcon Graphics, Helena, Montana

Distributed by Falcon Press Publishing Co., Inc. P.O. Box 1718, Helena, Montana 59624, or call 1-800-582-2665

D

edication:

To: Brianna, Conor,
 and Haydn...
My grandest gifts at
Christmastime
Are the looks of
 wonderment on my
 grandchildrens' faces
As short arms reach
 deep into
Christmas stockings;
 and to see the
Deserved pride shown
 by parents who know
 that their children are
 growing up well,
Just as they did.
                    G.D.S.

"Most all the time, the whole year long,
     there ain't no flies on me,
But jest 'fore Christmas, I'm as good as I kin be!"

                    "Just 'fore Christmas"
                    Eugene Field

Contents

The Sound Of Christmastime

Ben Foresgren began his work-day as principal of Kennedy Middle School with much the same routine as had been his custom for the last twenty-six years.

The night-light above the front door of the school fought through the December darkness and provided just enough illumination to select the right key from the many others on the metal ring. Inside the building, he shut the door and instinctively flipped the three light switches that lit up the hallway from one end of the school to the other.

Ben stood on the rubber mat in the entryway as he brushed a skiff of snow from the shoulders of his down jacket. He welcomed the warmth, while once again taking satisfaction in having arrived at school before Bernie, his custodian. A feeling of pride prompted an inward smile as he noted how nice the decorated hallway looked, bedecked in its holiday trimmings.

The walk to his office followed the normal path, although this morning he tried to be more careful, so as not to slip on the polished terrazzo floor. Inside the principal's office, Ben made his way past the reception counter and secretary's desk to the smaller room that had been both his school home and sanctuary for so long.

Having his own adjoining restroom was one of the few administrative perks his position afforded him. He hung his cap and jacket on the hook inside the door, then turned on the hot water tap of the 1930s vintage sink. He let the water warm up before dousing his face and wetting the too few hairs that had to be judiciously distributed to somewhat cover his baldness. His extended forehead shined back at him.

"You should get a hair piece," Bernie once told him. "It'll make you look younger."

To Ben, looking younger was not one of his primary goals. Being in sync with his soon-to-be-celebrated fifty-eighth birthday and trying to feel good about his life as a near senior citizen he considered more worthwhile ways to spend his time and energy. Besides, there seemed to be something synthetic, if not untruthful, about wearing a wig—even one that didn't stick out like an English riding saddle on a plow horse. *"It's more important to be who and what you are, old or not,"* Ben reminded himself.

After doing the best he could to comb his longer side hairs into place, Ben touched the tan age spot on his forehead. This had been a more recent memory marker to clearly establish that he was fast approaching the status of a modern day saber-toothed tiger, doomed to sink into the educational mire and become extinct.

He closed the restroom door, sighed, and made his way to his roll-top desk. It took only a slight pull with his index finger to slide the tambour upward. He had long ago stopped locking his desk at night. Why let some hoodlum pry the lock and ruin a fine antique, only to find a collection of pens, pencils, and paper clips? The most money ever left in his desk overnight was a couple of dollars in change that could be used to bail out a kid who forgot his lunch money.

As usual, he had cleared the top of the desk of yesterday's paper crises the night before. Now, nothing was in view but the edge of a manila filing folder, slightly too large to fit in the cubby hole where it had been stored.

Ben sat down in his chair and, pulling with his heels, rolled up to the desk. His eyes fixed on the protruding folder. For the second time this morning he softly sighed, then slid the folder onto the desktop. The act of starting his day by reviewing its contents was the only recently initiated difference in his otherwise established morning routine. The cover bore no title, but inside a yellow legal pad was headed ''Retirement—Pro and Con.''

Under the ''Pro'' side, the entries read:

1. Won't be taking any trip to Hawaii, but retirement check plus savings should be enough for Pauline and me to live on.

2. No more P.T.A. meetings,

3. or Retention Conferences,

4. or Child Study Teams,

5. or dreary meetings at the administration building,

6. or dealings with ''Gifted Parents,''

7. or bond levies.

8. We can do some traveling and see the kids more often.

9. Might even get away when the winter gets a bit too long in February.

The "Con" side contained an equal number of items:

1. We'll have to make some adjustments in lifestyle due to less income.

2. Will have to pay my own health insurance.

3. I'll miss the electricity and rebirth at the beginning of the school year,

4. and working with talented teachers,

5. and meeting a new batch of kids each year,

6. and watching them mature and grow,

7. and learn,

8. and taking pride that I am doing something important in life.

9. Will no longer be in a position to make educational decisions based on what I believe is the best thing for kids and teachers.

A voice behind him caused Ben to quickly close the folder.

"Whatcha workin' on?" Bernie asked.

The custodian moved closer to pick up the waste-basket, while attempting to look over Ben's shoulder.

"Nothing too important. Just reviewing my stock portfolio." Ben allowed himself a half-smile. "It's a real problem to know when to make a major investment with the market being as volatile as it is." He looked up at the custodian. "What do you think? Should I sell my IBM and buy utilities?"

"Hummph." Bernie carried the wastebasket to the canvas sack mounted on his cart. "With my salary, how would I know about stock market stuff? The BM in IBM might as well mean bowel movement for all I know. But if I made as much dough as you and the teachers do. . . ."

Ben made a clicking sound with his tongue. "Yes, it sure is a problem. Having too much money is almost as bad as not having enough. You don't want to leave it lying around without getting a maximum yield."

Bernie cleared his throat again, noisily dropped the wastebasket on the floor, then busied himself dusting the window sill.

Ben had been playing this game with Bernie for some years now. It started after he caught his custodian going through the teachers' mailboxes and making a list of their salaries from the withholding slips. That incident, or the resultant letter of reprimand that was placed in his personnel file, were never again mentioned by either of them. Bernie did, however, never miss the opportunity to complain, to anyone who would listen, that he had to "work twelve months a year to make a living, while the teachers get three months off."

Ben once again reminded himself that Bernie certainly kept the school clean and took as much pride in its appearance as he did. *"And I guess that's what's important,"* he thought.

"Oh, I almost forgot." Bernie walked back toward the desk. "Remember last year when I told you that Miss Rodgers made a mess on the stage with her Christmas program and all? You know, some paint spots and scratches in the stage? Well, she's doing it again this year."

Ben slowly turned his chair around and squinted over the top of his glasses. "Melody is one of the finest teachers in this district, and she goes an extra mile in taking responsibility for the Christmas programs each year. I can think of no one in this building who does more for kids than she does."

"Well, anyway," Bernie turned away and reached high to dust the top of the door trim. "It got better after I told you about it last year. Will you at least do what you did then?"

"Since you feel that that was the right thing to do, I'll give you my word that I'll do exactly what I did last year." The image of the word *"nothing"* came clearly to mind. His half-smile returned.

"Good. Appreciate it. Have a nice day." He folded his dust cloth and left. Ben heard him whistling, "We Wish You a Merry Christmas," as the cart rolled through the outer office.

Ben reopened his retirement folder and added one entry to each column. Under "Pro," he wrote, "10. I won't have to justify my salary to school critics." Below "Con," he added "10. Won't get the chance to zing Bernie anymore."

The hexagonal Regulator clock on the wall clicked onto 7:30. He put his elbow on the desk and rested his chin on his hand. Although his pen was still at the ready position, he could muster up no additional items for his lists. Instead, he just stared at the clock waiting for it to jerk ahead another minute. There was still half an hour to wait before the kids and teachers would arrive.

Outside his office, Melody Rodgers' laughter provided

a welcome relief from his melancholy. She has a verve for life, as well as for teaching, and the type of personality that attracts students to her in a way that would make the Pied Piper envious.

"Hey, Mr. Foresgren" echoed through the outer office. "Come on out here and see what these two characters have conjured up now."

The teacher wore a pair of much-too-large coveralls, which undoubtedly protected her designer jeans and one of her always-stylish sweaters. She was arranging some construction paper cutouts on the top of the reception counter while her two students proudly looked on. A forlorn Santa Claus started to take shape.

"Since this is my week for the hall bulletin board, and being up to my ears with the Christmas program, I asked Carlos and Sarah to bail me out and come up with something unique."

Ben smiled down at the Hispanic student, then raised his right hand to tediously sign the letters: H-I C-A-R-L-O-S.

The boy responded with a flourish of hand and finger movement.

Carlos was a non-speaking student who, according to his speech therapists, could hear and had no physical disability that prohibited him from speaking. He merely refused to talk and had done so for as long as anybody remembered.

"Hold on, now." The principal raised his hand, palm forward. "You're going too fast for a person with my kind of reading problem. What did he say, Sarah?"

The slender girl lowered her eyes and bit her lip. She put her hands behind her back and sadly stood unmoving until Carlos nudged her with his elbow and tipped his head toward Ben.

Sarah finally answered, "He said, 'Merry Christmas, Mr. Principal.' "

Ben nodded and gave Carlos a pat on the back. "And a Merry Christmas to you and your very special friend, Sarah." He winked at the girl, and she seemed a bit more at ease.

Melody Rodgers continued to lay out the pieces of construction paper. "It's coming," she said, "but you won't believe it."

The saddened Santa stood with his hands on his hips, looking down at his sleigh piled high with presents. Its reins rested unattached on the ground. Each of the reindeer, even the red-nosed Rudolph, hung upside down by their back legs. One could not help but notice the red tongues sticking sideways out of the reindeers' mouths.

Sarah seemed more at ease now as she and Carlos arranged the letters above the scene: SHOT DURING HUNTING SEASON. The two students stepped back and waited for their principal's assessment.

Ben's laughter filled the office. "You bet. Absolutely top notch. This has to be the most unique bulletin board this old school has ever seen. It'll sure get everyone's attention, and I'll bet we have a traffic jam around it when the rest of the kids get to school." He turned to Miss Rodgers. "You sure picked the right artists for this job."

The teacher hugged her students. "See, I told you he'd like it. Now, I'd better leave you two to tack it up, while I get back to the auditorium. If I don't get crackin', there's no way our show's going to come off on schedule. Only three more days, and we haven't even finished the manger yet."

At the sound of the word "manger" Ben's internal alarm system emitted a faint beep. It had been a stronger and louder signal when Melody first informed him that her students voted to use the traditional Christmas story for their program this year, complete with carols and creche.

He made sure that Sarah and Carlos saw him slowly sign C-O-N-G-R-A-T-U-L-A-T-I-O-N-S O-N A G-O-O-D J-O-B before he returned to his office.

Again at his desk, Ben assured himself that if it had been any teacher other than Melody Rodgers, he would have dissuaded her from embarking on such a sensitive journey. He was well aware of the "Winter Wolves," whose howls chilled even the most supportive school board members. Within the past two years, he had weathered the critics' objections to having Judy Blume books in the library, as well as answering the outcry made by a vocal church group that school Halloween parties were furthering the cause of Satanism. If this year was to be his last at Kennedy School, he didn't really need another public furor for a preretirement going-away gift.

But Melody Rodgers was different. In her five years in this building, she had single-handedly written, organized, directed, and played the musical accompaniment for the yearly Christmas programs. She also had a special way of bringing out the best in her students, and caused each to feel extra proud of the contribution made to the program's success. The parents couldn't be more pleased, and Bernie's minor complaints were the only voiced criticisms he had ever heard. His guiding principle in matters like this was "Get out of a talented teacher's way, then take some of the undeserved credit for the good things that happen to the children."

The eight o'clock bell brought Ben back to reality and provided the opportunity to welcome the excitement that children bring to another school day. He tucked the folder back in its place and closed the sliding tambour before heading for the knot of early-arriving children who would be lined up outside the front door.

He knew that the next hour would pass rapidly. After being sure that the kids had some semblance of order as they filed into the school, he made his way throughout the building giving "Good mornings" to each of the teachers and asking if he could be of any help to them.

He saved the visit to the auditorium until last. It was his "dessert" to watch Melody Rodgers orchestrate the organized chaos in preparation for the upcoming program. As expected, a din of busy noises filled the room as clusters of children worked independently on their assigned tasks. Student directors presided over each work group, while the teacher flitted from one part of the room to the other.

The singers who surrounded the piano were accompanied by a little girl one-fingering "Hark the Herald Angels Sing." Only a few of the actors wore some part of their costumes—a crown or bathrobe—to separate kings from shepherds. Part of the set crew banged the stable together, while one boy stretched high atop a ladder to hang the electric star. All together, the class created a cacophony that was music to Ben's ears. He begrudgingly waved goodbye to Miss Rodgers before leaving.

As he entered the office, his secretary put her hand over the telephone mouthpiece. "It's for you." Then whispered, "Your first irate parent, and it's not even nine o'clock yet."

Ben closed his door, then took enough time to settle into his chair and prop his right foot on a lower desk drawer before picking up the receiver. "This is Mr. Foresgren, how may I help you?"

After a brief pause, the strained voice at the other end of the line answered, "You can help me by teaching basic skills in your school instead of proselytizing the students."

"That sounds like a good idea." Ben tried to keep an unthreatened tone in his voice. "But first, I need to know to whom I'm speaking, and I guess you'll have to be more specific as to what we've done to upset you."

The voice breathed heavily into the phone. "This is Arthur Spooner. I have a daughter, Sarah, in Kennedy School."

Ben interrupted, "Sarah? I just spoke to her and Carlos earlier this morning. I can't imagine Sarah having a problem. She's one of the nicest young ladies in the seventh grade. Come to think of it, though, she didn't seem to be her normal happy self. Is she feeling all right?"

"No, she isn't feeling all right, and that's why I'm calling. It's the unconscionable actions of one of your teachers that's causing the trouble."

"And which teacher is that?" Ben reached for a notepad.

"I think her name is Rodgers. And I can't believe that you would allow one of your staff members to defy the Constitution and impose her personal religious beliefs on a group of impressionable children in a tax-supported school."

Now it was Ben's turn to use a few seconds to try to phrase a response. While doing so, the electronic monotone in his mind beeped on, "I tried to warn you. Why didn't you listen to me?"

Although he knew the answer to his own question, Ben asked, "Have you talked to Miss Rodgers about your concerns? If not, I'd be willing to arrange a conference so that you two can sit down and see if this matter can be resolved in an objective manner."

"You're missing the point." The voice raised in intensity. "I don't intend to talk to Miss Rodgers. Nor will you mention my name in connection with this complaint. She seems to have some charismatic hold on my daughter that has already caused enough grief. You're the principal. It's your responsibility to put a stop to sectarian activities in your school. Besides, I don't want the teacher taking it out on my daughter."

Again, Ben waited a moment before responding. "Mr. Spooner, first, let me assure you that Melody Rodgers is not the kind of person who would be biased against any student, especially someone as nice as Sarah. Second, if you wish for me to take any action on your complaint, you must agree to speak to the teacher. That's just the way I've handled matters like this for the last twenty-six years, and I don't intend to change now. I would, however, be willing to be present during the conference if you and Miss Rodgers wish me to be there."

An extended period of silence followed, and Ben wondered if the parent had hung up the phone. Finally, the voice said, "All right. But I want to get this settled as soon as possible. No later than today. Have no doubt, I am deadly serious and intend to pursue this with your superintendent if I can't gain your cooperation."

"Let's see...," Ben pretended to be checking the class schedule, although he knew it well from memory. "Miss Rodgers has a planning period at 1:10. We'll meet in my office, if that time is convenient for you and Mrs. Spooner."

"There is no longer a Mrs. Spooner, and absolutely nothing about this whole affair is convenient." The phone clicked off.

Ben took out a new writing tablet and headed the first page "A Visit from Santa." The first two entries were easy. "1. Call the supt. and brief him on the situation. 2. Find a school law book and read up on religion in the school."

"Still working on your investment stuff?" Bernie leaned against the doorway.

Ben didn't look up. "No. This time it's school business." He concentrated on the blank line following the number 3.

Bernie shrugged. "Well, I figured that since the building's going to be in such a mess this week, I'd treat myself to a cup of downtown coffee. Maybe a roll, too. So would you watch things here while I'm gone? With all the candy some of those kids eat this time of year, there'll probably be at least one spit-up while I'm out."

The principal nodded, still not taking his eyes off the yellow pad. "Sure, I'll take care of it." Ben rubbed at his eyes. He wanted to add that *"cleaning up your kind of mess would be much easier than the one I have to face this afternoon."*

Bernie turned to leave. "See you later then, in 'bout a half'n hour."

Number 3 became: "Alert Melody about conference, but not until noon. No need to bother her during classtime." Since no number 4 came to mind, he reluctantly closed the door and dialed the superintendent's number at the administration building. The call turned out to be less of a problem than he expected. His boss had already left town and would not be back until January. He drew a line through the first entry.

Ben opened the sliding glass door of the top oak bookcase. Starting at the left side, he moved his index finger along the the row of books until coming to a blue-backed volume titled *Law in the Schools, Second Edition.*

He removed it and the paperback next to it, then returned to his desk. The smaller text looked far less imposing, but had a copyright date four years earlier than the heavier book. Before starting his review, he took a light blue felt-tipped pen from his top drawer and tested it on the yellow writing pad. The shade of green that resulted matched his disposition.

As expected, each text contained a pertinent section. Chapter 5 of the smaller book was headed "Religious Activities in Public Schools" and Chapter 4 of the blueback was "Religion and Public Education." Ben shrugged. *"Enough for a quick and dirty refresher course. Should at least have the milestone cases and elementary principles for elementary principals."*

Opening the smaller book, he sensed that the office was much warmer now, but not hot enough to cause the perspiration that beaded on his forehead. He closed the book. It would take another trip to the restroom before he was ready for his required reading.

Ben watched the clock click down onto 1:04. What lunch he had managed to eat sat undigested in his stomach. He wished Melody would have arrived earlier, so that they could have some time to plan their strategy. Irate parents are seldom late.

The teacher was still panting as she shut the door and plunked herself down on one of the two chairs that had been brought in from the outer office. "Sorry I couldn't get here sooner. I had some kids coming in to work and needed to get things organized so that they could carry on while I was gone. I'll bet you didn't need a problem like this to round out your day."

He made an effort to look as unruffled as possible. "Look, Melody, I don't want you getting all upset over this thing. You're the best I've got, so I know it's going to work itself out just fine."

The teacher managed a weak smile.

Ben leaned back in his chair. "In situations like this, I've found that it's best to give the parent plenty of time to get whatever's bothering him off his chest. It's kind of like a phonograph record that needs to be played out before it can eject. So neither of us will say any more than we have to for at least . . . five minutes.

When I sense he's run his course, I'll call on you to merely tell your side of the story. I'll preside over the conference, but you'll represent the school."

His secretary buzzed to signal the parent's arrival exactly as the clock ticked to 1:10. Ben opened the door and extended his hand. "Mr. Spooner, I'm Ben Foresgren. Come on in." The parent hesitantly returned the handshake.

Before he had the opportunity to introduce her, Melody stood up and warmly smiled at the parent. "I'm Melody Rodgers, and now I finally get the chance to meet Sarah's dad. Since I must have missed you at Open House, I've been wanting to tell you how fortunate I feel to have Sarah in my homeroom."

Arthur Spooner cleared his throat. "Hmmph. I often have to work nights." He quickly looked away and sat down.

Ben rotated his chair to face the parent. "I want to sincerely thank you for taking time off to come to school. I've found that when teachers and parents get together, it almost always benefits the student. But, being as busy as I know you must be at this time of year, why don't we start by having you express your concerns to Miss Rodgers?"

Mr. Spooner took a deep breath, then looked directly at Ben. "Before we start, I want you to know that I'm not a chronic school critic. As point of fact, this is the first time I've felt it necessary to complain about one of my daughter's teachers."

Ben nodded, then tactfully pointed toward Melody in an effort to encourage him to direct his remarks to her.

"But when a school, or teacher, surrounds children with religious sectarianism, totally ignoring the wall that separates church and state, my conscience compels me to raise a serious objection."

He paused, undoubtedly waiting for a denial. When neither the principal or teacher spoke, he continued. "What makes this especially unthinkable, is that you can't pick up a newspaper without reading some account of another raging conflict between Christian and Muslim, or Jews fighting both of them, or the Irish blowing each other up. All this in the name of some archaic, organized religion."

He hesitated long enough to catch his breath. "Establishment." He glared at Ben. "You must be aware of the First Amendment provision that restricts a public, tax-supported agency from the establishment of a religion."

Ben broke his own self-imposed rule of silence. "Or from prohibiting the free exercise of that religion." The moment he heard his own voice, he knew it would have been better to wait the five minutes.

"Oh, come on now. Don't tell me that you're going to try to defend subjecting my immature daughter to your religious dogma. If she were in college, she could get up and walk out of a class. But you don't do that when you're a seventh grade student. Immaculate Conception. Burning bushes. Goodwill toward men. Stars that lead the Magi. Astrological bunk."

Although he was tempted to dispute the point, Ben allowed himself but one word, "Oh?" then leaned back in his chair.

Silence filled the small room until the clock moved

up one more minute. *"That's five,"* Ben thought.

"Mr. Spooner, rather than an argument, or even a defense of our position, I believe you should allow Miss Rodgers to merely explain how the decision to hold a more traditional Christmas program came about. Melody."

Before starting to speak, the teacher swallowed once, then sat as tall as she could. "Well, right or wrong, I always let the kids select their own program. I've found that they work harder and take more pride when they've had a voice in the selection. This year I've got an especially talented group, and when I presented some alternatives to them, one of them proposed that we write our own version of the original Christmas story. The other kids chimed in, and when the vote was taken I thought it was unanimous." She momentarily lowered her eyes. "I guess I was mistaken."

Ben readjusted his sitting position. *"Mistaken? I doubt it. Trying to avoid family conflicts would be more believable,"* he thought.

Mr. Spooner stiffened. "Sarah wouldn't vote for a sectarian theme. She knows how I feel."

"Of course." Melody nodded. "I should have sensed that when she asked to work with Carlos on the hall bulletin board, rather than have a part in the program. I remember telling her how much we'd miss her beautiful singing voice, but I probably assumed that she just wanted to help her friend. That's another thing I wanted to tell you, how much I appreciate Sarah's help with Carlos. I don't know what I'd have done this year without her. I hope this

situation won't interfere with their special friendship."
She reached over and touched the parent's hand.

He quickly withdrew his arm. "It shouldn't. They
both have something in common. Neither has a mother.
Something happened to Mrs. Sanchez when her family
was illegally crossing the border. Sarah's 'so called'
mother left her four years ago during this joyous
Holiday Season."

Miss Rodgers said softly, "I really appreciate your
telling me. . .about their mothers. It must be pretty hard
to be a single parent, especially at this time of year. I'm
sorry."

"Don't be. We're doing all right, in spite of situations
like this that keep disrupting our family." He glanced
up at the clock, then glared at Ben. "I think there's been
enough said, and I really have to get back to work. So,
what's it going to be? Are you going to meet your
constitutional responsibility and leave religiosity to the
churches, or am I going to have to go over your head
on this matter?"

Ben had had plenty of time to prethink his response.
"When you came into the office earlier this afternoon,
you wanted to make sure we realized that you were
not a chronic complainer. After hearing you out, I
believe you. Nor do I question your sincerity or
motivation in raising your objections. Now, I hope you
believe me when I tell you that both Miss Rodgers and
I deeply care about Sarah. You should be very proud
of your daughter. I know I would be, if I were her
father."

He paused before continuing. "I'd be less than honest
if I didn't also say that I'm equally concerned with the

welfare of the many other students who are fortunate enough to have Miss Rodgers for their teacher."

The parent sat rigidly in his chair while the teacher bit at a fingernail.

"As to your objections based on constitutional doctrine, I guess I'm not near as sure you are that a public school Christmas program either advances, or inhibits a religious belief. Although I'm certainly no lawyer, my reading has led me to believe that, in objections like this, the legal outcome has been as much dependent on particular circumstances as general principle. So where does that leave us? No doubt, with a hard problem. Miss Rodgers and I will discuss this matter, and I'll promise to call you back later this afternoon, after we've had time to consider what's best for all the children."

"That's not good enough." Although Mr. Spooner didn't raise his voice, the stress was apparent. "You asked me to take off work and come down here, and I did. Now, I believe I deserve a decision."

Miss Rodgers' eyes opened as wide as possible.

Ben nodded once. "Okay. I've never had much trouble making decisions. The program will take place as scheduled. However, I shall leave it totally up to Miss Rodgers as to what it will be, and she'll have my total support. After working with her for five years, I can assure you that she will be especially cognizant of your feelings and would do nothing to hurt your daughter. And oh yes, you might, or might not, have heard that this may be my last year as principal of Kennedy School. If so, I could hardly be concerned as to whether or not you go over my head."

Arthur Spooner bit down hard. "All right. But you should know that I plan to be in attendance at the program, and if I hear one word, sung or spoken, of a religious nature, I shall raise an objection that could make your last year a problem-filled one." He got up and left the office.

Ben had expected Melody to be noticeably upset. Instead, her mouth turned up in a wry smile and she seemed to have unusual twinkle in her eyes. Then her mood sobered. "Did you really mean what you said?"

"Never been surer. You'll do what's best for the kids. I know that."

"No, I mean, you're not really going to retire, are you?"

"Maybe. But, my retirement has nothing to do with our situation today. Except that if I do decide to bag it after this year, I sure won't miss dealing with human problems that are too complicated for humans to solve." Ben stood up. "Now, I know you want to get back to work. The next couple of days should tax even your storehouse of creative energy."

Melody started to leave, then stopped in the doorway. "Happy Winter Holiday, Boss. Does that sound better than 'Merry Christmas?' "

The rest of the week was filled to overflowing with the anticipated ado leading up to the last day of school. Ben had little unused time to worry about the outcome of the parent's threat. Friday was now upon him, and the kids were sky high. Visions of Christmas trees, presents with fancy bows, and a fat man ho-ho-hoing down the chimney relegated class-room instruction to far-distant second place.

For the last two days, Ben purposely avoided stopping in the auditorium during his morning trips around the school. He didn't want to seem to be prying or unsupportive of Melody's decisions.

He watched the parents file past his office, chuckle at the bulletin board, then scurry down the hallway in hopes of getting a seat in the auditorium good enough to be seen by their children. Though he tried to fend it off, a feeling of uneasiness prompted both a stom-ach ache and an Excedrin headache. During other years, he welcomed the tiredness of this last afternoon, knowing that a break from his duties was well in sight.

His discomfort increased when he noticed that Bernie had chosen the worst possible time to mop the hallway directly in front of the auditorium door. Parents were bunched together, waiting for their turn to skirt the watered down terrazzo. Teachers tried vainly to maintain discipline as their classes lined up along the walls.

Ben politely "excused" his way through the crowd. "Bernie—"

"I know, you want me to finish up, so's the people can get inside." He poked his mop into the bucket, spilling some of the soapy water on the recently scrubbed floor.

"I just don't want 'em tracking their mud in there. You know, we'd be a whole lot better off without these Christmas programs. Dismiss schools a half day earlier. Whew." He picked up the bucket with one hand, while wiping imaginary sweat from his brow with the other.

A stern "Coming through" parted the Red Sea of school patrons. Bernie chugged down the hallway muttering to himself.

Ben stepped aside to let the knot of parents unravel. He slightly shook his head. *"Could it possibly be that the Bernies and Arthur Spooners of this world are right and I've been wrong all these years?"*

Inside the auditorium, the moment of self-doubt quickly faded. He found himself engulfed in the Sound of Christmastime. Parents happily chatted with each other, pleased to have found seats in the center section or front rows. The students seated in the back of room, and on the extreme sides, knew well that this program signaled the end of school and the beginning of their forthcoming vacation. Despite menacing looks from homeroom teachers, they made but a half-hearted effort to hold back titters and giggles.

The chorus of Santa's elves formed a crescent around the piano, in front of the right side of the stage. Their stocking caps, red-rouged cheeks, T-shirts, and gym trunks over every imaginable color of leotards added to the gaily decorated auditorium. The singers buzzed with excitement and their chins stretched high to get a glimpse of a relative or parent. Ben spotted Sarah seated in the front row before the choir, but not part of it.

At least every other second, a new face peeked through the center split in the stage curtains. A podium stood at the corner of the stage, right above the singers. *"But where's the microphone?"* Ben wondered.

Even the back rows were almost filled, yet people continued to file in. Ben busied himself by directing some of the late arrivers to vacant seats scattered throughout the auditorium. When he saw Mr. Spooner come in, he pointed to an empty chair. The parent merely shook his head and moved to the far corner of the room. Ben walked to the doorway and stood with the dozen or so other standing-room-only patrons.

The lights dimmed and a spotlight scanned the broad smiles of the choir of elves. Last minute audience whispers subsided as the piano tinkled the introduction to "Deck the Halls." Instead of the crystal clear voices, the chorus softly hummed the melody. Each verse ended with a more spirited "Tra-la-la-la-la." As Santa's helpers slowed to finish the song with an especially exuberant "La-la-la-la-la, la-la, la, laaaaa," the spotlight shifted upward and fixed on the speakerless podium.

A wide-eyed Carlos, wearing a broad-brimmed sombrero, entered from the side of the stage and stepped up on a box behind the speaking stand. A hush fell over the room as he shaded his eyes, searching the front row seats. Ben saw Sarah inconspicuously raise her hand and form a circle with her thumb and forefinger. The boy beamed as he faced the audience and slowly signed what must have been a welcome to Kennedy School. Then like a circus ringmaster, he dramatically swept his arm toward the center of the stage. The curtains opened with a series of jerks, revealing the dimly lit set. The two-by-four stable that Ben remembered, had been sheeted with cardboard and topped with a red-lettered sign—'STARDUST MOTEL." A square opening at the end of the building bore a smaller "garage" label.

The star was still there, but was unlit. Scrap paper

snow wafted down, although every once in a while, a whole handful dropped heavily from above. The choir hummed "Winter Wonderland."

The snow finally stopped, and two grey-haired, middle school students came out of the motel and looked up at the sign. The man wore blue bib overalls while his wife had an apron on over her long dress. The spotlight on Carlos narrowed until it primarily focused on his hands and face. He smiled broadly as he started to tell his story. Though he undoubtedly tried to go as slow as possible, he could not help but speed up when the man sent his wife back inside the cardboard structure.

The star first blinked on and off, then shined brightly above the Stardust Motel. When the woman came back outside to hold her husband's arm, Carlos seemed as proud as they were. His hand movements and expressions welcomed each of the customers that came from stage left, entered the office, then exited stage right carrying red-tagged keys. Finally, the old man came out and hung a "No Vacancy" sign beside the doorway. A few people were turned away. Carlos and the manager faced the audience and hunched their shoulders at the same time.

It was then that the young man and his pregnant wife arrived. Ben recognized the girl with the pillow strapped beneath her coat. He knew, too, that her mother had recently presented her family with a new baby brother. No doubt, the girl learned to lean back and waddle across the stage by watching her mother.

Even in the darkened auditorium, Ben noticed the smiles throughout the audience. Some of the students gave their friends elbow nudges and knowing looks. He took a quick glance at Mr. Spooner, who seemed stoically unmoved by the scene.

Carlos sadly shook his head as the manager mimed his regret in having "no room in the inn." The narrator perked up and his movements directed the audience to notice the wife tug on her husband's overalls, then point to the garage at the end of the motel.

While Carlos' gestures told of the apologetic offer by the motel keeper, the husband ushered the mother-to-be into the garage. The stage darkened, leaving the star shining brightly as the choir whistled "Christmas Blues," a song Ben had heard on a Willie Nelson record.

The scene warmed as a new light was turned on inside the garage. Carlos moved back to let the birth scene unfold without dialogue. The father and his pillowless wife knelt beside a white wicker bassinet, while their hosts leaned against the garage doorway.

The procession that followed was led by two cowboys. One held the reins of a red-nosed, four-legged "horse" with an army blanket body and a brown, paper bag head. The other wore a black patch over one eye and swaggered across the stage with a definite John Wayne gait. Each placed a gift by the bassinet, then stood in the background.

The next character caused all in the audience to stretch for a better view of the stage. A boy with slicked back hair, wearing a black leather jacket lettered "King of Rock and Roll," strummed his guitar as he gyrated across the stage. He put a record beside the crib. Then a girl in a Sacramento Kings sweatsuit dribbled a basketball to the garage and put it next to the record.

Finally, a caped, chubby boy in a crown preceded three girls carrying violins. This king's lunch pail became the final gift.

It started to snow again as the choir "loo-loo-loo'd" their way through "White Christmas." The actors strained to hold their assigned positions and remain in character until the song ended.

Carlos stepped back into the spotlight and pointed to each set of characters as he concluded telling his story. He then lowered his head as the curtains slowly pulled together. As soon as the gap closed, a cheer went up back stage, and the curtains were again reeled back.

The audience enthusiastically applauded as actors dodged in and out to form a line. Carlos hopped down from his box and, after acknowledging the singers, summoned first the kings, then the cowboys, to center stage. The motel manager and his wife received a little more applause, but when the father and mother came forward carrying a Cabbage Patch Doll, everyone stood up and clapped even louder.

Carlos held up both hands to urge the parents to again sit down. Since many in the audience were now putting on their coats, the other actors prompted their attention by also moving their hands up and down. Some ssh'd their moms and dads back into their seats.

When he regained control, Carlos sent the two cowboys off stage. They returned arm-in-arm with Miss Rodgers, still dressed in her paint-spattered coveralls. Carlos motioned for them to bring the teacher over to the podium. After the other players gathered around, he stepped back up on his box and retrieved a plastic container from under the stand. Removing the corsage, he started to pin it on his teacher. The pin prick startled not only Miss Rogers, but her yelp surprised everyone else on the stage.

An embarrassed master of ceremonies slapped his forehead, then raised one finger to ask the audience to bear with him for at least one more minute. He ran down the stairs at the edge of the stage and pulled a reluctant Sarah Spooner back with him. The other children all cheered as he handed the corsage and pin to his friend.

Sarah took a quick look toward the back of the room, then stepped up on the box to pin on the corsage. This time the audience joined the cast in showing their appreciation.

Miss Rodgers threw a kiss to the singers and actors before giving Carlos a big hug. Still up on the box, Sarah leaned over and whispered in her teacher's ear. This time, it was Melody who signaled for quiet. Sarah stepped down and stood by Carlos.

All eyes were on the boy as he removed his sombrero and stood twisting its brim. His face reddened and he pursed his lips. "Mmmmmm, ugh."

He took a deep breath, blew it out and tried again. "Mmmmmm...ugh...errrr...eee." He smiled at Sarah. "Mm-airrr-eee Kah-risss-muss." The stage erupted with everyone patting him on the back and giving him "high fives." Melody Rodgers' shoulders sagged as she wiped at her cheek with her shirt sleeve. Ben saw Mr. Sanchez hurriedly wend his way to the stage. *"Now that's got to be the most beautiful Christmas sound I've ever heard,"* Ben thought.

Ben stopped in the auditorium doorway, accepting

the many undeserved compliments he had expected. "Great show." "Best program ever, and I've had four kids go to school here." "Congratulations, Mr. Foresgren. You must be very proud of the children." "My son was Elvis. Wasn't that something?"

Arthur Spooner waited until the room was almost empty before approaching the principal. "Okay, I'll give you this one. But I still feel the same way about the separation of schools and religion." He offered Ben his hand.

Ben warmly accepted the handshake. "I'm sure you do, Arthur. I guess that's what makes our country so great. We don't have to kill each other just because we see things differently."

The parent dropped his hand to his side, then shifted his weight from one foot to the other. "Uh. I have to admit that your Miss Rodgers does one whale of a job with kids. Something very nice happened to both Sarah and Carlos today. You might let her know that I'm appreciative."

"Sure, I'll do that; but I know she'd rather hear it from you." Ben watched him walk away. He was especially pleased to see Sarah join her dad and walk hand-in-hand with him toward the exit.

Ben felt almost numb as he sat at his desk. It was dark outside and the school was quiet now. Although so many students stopped by to wish him a Merry Christmas, each greeting was appreciated. A weary group of teachers had been sent on their way with final paychecks and a special thank you from their principal. He opened his retirement folder and picked up his pen.

"Still at it, huh?" Bernie pushed his dustmop inside the office. "You know, next year I might ask you to give me some advice on playing the market."

Ben allowed himself a weak smile. "It's pretty risky. Are you sure you want to jump in?"

"Why not? You look like you're doing real good." He swept himself through the doorway.

"Yes," Ben said to the custodian's back. "I'm doing just fine. Merry Christmas, Bernie. And Happy New Year."

"Same to you," echoed back.

Ben wrote one more item to the list under "Con": "11. When I retire, I'll dearly miss the Sound of Christmastime."

Without a Home at Christmastime

Even the indoor warmth and shelter from the swirling blizzard did little to bolster his spirits. Rob Newton walked down the carpeted hallway of the office building and stopped outside the full-length glass panel of the lighted doorway. He moved to one side so he could get a better look at his reflected image without having the gold-painted letters block out his face.

He stood unmoving as he silently mouthed the words, "Adult Probation and Parole Bureau." It wasn't the "Probation" part of the title that bothered him the most. After all, he knew well why he was required to report to the probation officer. It was the word "Adult" that didn't set right in his internal assessment system. When you've just barely turned eighteen, you only think of yourself as an adult when someone wants to treat you as a juvenile.

Rob took longer than necessary to wipe his feet, unsling his bookbag, brush the snow from his jacket, and slap his out-of-season Giants baseball cap against his Levis. Then taking a deep breath, he turned the brass doorknob and entered the too-small outer office.

The middle-aged secretary looked up from her computer keyboard. "Hi, handsome. How's my favorite soon-to-be-discovered, world-class artist making it this holiday season?"

Rob forced a half-smile. "I'm doing okay, Irma. Not great, but at least okay. Thanks for asking."

He set his bookbag on the floor and looked over his shoulder. "Is Bernie busy? He called the dorm last night and said he wanted to see me this morning."

Irma glanced down at the blinking red light on her telephone. "I'm sure he won't be too long. He's on the..."

The voice from the farthest office raised in intensity. "Well, I guess I'm disappointed that you and your husband feel this way, Mrs. Newton. Just permitting Rob to return for Christmas isn't good enough. It's been a year now and in my opinion he's made a world of progress. I don't want him to take a giant step backward. It would be better for him to stay here than to feel unwanted in his own home."

The secretary stood up and touched Rob's hand before walking to the probation officer's room. As she started to close the door, Rob heard Bernie's lower tone of voice. "Yes, there's probably nothing more either of us can say, except that I'm sorry, too."

Irma took Rob by the arm and moved him toward the waiting room. "Hey, I think we've got a new *Sports Illustrated* in here if some bozo hasn't already swiped it. It's not the swimsuit issue, that's for sure. That lasted for less than a day before vanishing into thin air."

He sat down on one of the two well-worn couches

while the secretary shuffled through a pile of magazines on the coffee table. "Here it is." Irma held the *Sports Illustrated* in front of him and slapped the front cover with the back of her hand. "Features a rundown of the upcoming bowl games. Not bad, huh?"

Rob nodded and accepted the offered magazine. He thumbed through the first few pages, trying to look interested.

The secretary started to walk out the door, then turned back and added, "I'll check and see if Bernie's off the phone. Would offer you a cup of coffee, but know you don't drink the stuff."

Alone in the waiting room, Rob placed the magazine down on the couch. He looked around the room to see if there was a new poster tacked on the wall since his last visit.

The three "No Smoking" signs and the card that urged him to "Register with Selective Service" were still in their same places, but the posters seemed different to him. One showed a cat half-buried in a snowbank. The caption below read, "Everyone makes mistakes. Mine was getting up this morning."

"Yeah, tell me about it," Rob mumbled as he unzipped his bookbag and took out a spiral-bound sketchbook. Opening to a blank page, he printed out the first message, then closed his eyes and tried to create a mental image that went along with the truism.

His probation officer's voice brought him back to reality. "I wish I had your talent in art. It must be great to have something productive to do when you have some time to fill."

Rob closed his sketchbook and looked over at the

slightly-built man leaning against the doorframe. He stood up and accepted Bernie's warm handshake. "I'm not sure talent is the right word to describe my drawings. My university art teacher is not that impressed with my work. Says it's illustrative and looks too much like a photograph."

Bernie shrugged, then said as they left the waiting room, "Well, 'to each his own,' the fellow said, as he kissed the pig."

This time Rob didn't have to force the smile. In his office, the probation officer gestured for him to sit in one of the two chairs in front of his desk while he sat in the other one. "Talking about school, how are things going up on the hill?" Bernie rested his elbow on the arm of the chair and leaned forward.

Rob shifted his position twice before he felt comfortable. "I guess, all things considered, it's going pretty good. Starting in January, I only have to report to the Dean of Students once a month. As to my coursework, I'm doing better in some classes than others, but I've been told that's normal. You know, when I started fall quarter, I thought I'd like my art class the best. As it turned out, I'm enjoying my logic course the most."

Bernie sat erect. "Is that a fact? Logic? When I was in college, I grooved on some of my philosophy classes, but avoided logic like an overdue bill. Do you think it's the teacher or the subject that makes it a good class?"

"I suppose it's some of both. The instructor seems to care about each of us and she sure does explain things well. But the most important thing I get out of

class is recognizing some of the fallacious reasoning
I've used in my life. Hopefully, this class will help me
get rid of some of my stinkin' thinkin'."

Bernie sat back and nodded. "Yeah. Me and a lot
of other people I know could benefit from lessons on
that subject." Then he leaned forward again and said
softly, "This morning, I talked to your mom. You know,
about going home for Christmas. She. . ."

"I'd rather stay here anyway. But I do have to get
out of the dorm by tomorrow night. They're closing
it down so the employees can at least have Christmas
weekend off." Rob looked down at his hands and
picked at a hangnail on his thumb.

Bernie waited for a moment before continuing.
"Sure, I can understand how you feel. You probably
want to avoid trouble. And I guess I can sort of understand how your folks might think it's the wrong time
of year for reconciliation. But with the way you've
been handling things now, it'll come. Might just take
a little longer, that's all."

"Uh huh." Rob pulled at his sweater collar and again
shifted his sitting position.

Bernie bent lower to gain eye contact with Rob. "I
do have a Plan B for a way to spend Christmas, if
you're interested."

A voice behind them caused both men to sit erect
and look back at the doorway. "Good morning, sport
fans."

Rob saw Irma outside, glaring at the man. Bernie's
eyes narrowed. "Marvin, can't you see we're having
a conference?"

"Now don't get so uptight with your down-the-hall

buddy. Loosen up. It's only two more days till ho ho ho time, and business has been pretty good this year. Besides, I just heard a cute little story that you'll get a kick out of." He stepped to the side and motioned with his head. "Come on in, Irm. This is okay for mixed company. It'll brighten up your day."

Bernie stood up. "Look, I have neither the time nor inclination to. . ."

Marvin put his arm around the probation officer. "Anyway, this Jewish kid went up to his father and said, 'Dad, would you lend me five dollars?' " He chuckled to himself. "And the Heeb said, 'Four dollars? What do you want three dollars for?' "

He looked from face to face for validation. When no one smiled, he moved next to Rob and nudged him with his elbow. "Don't you get it, kid? He asked for five and his father jewed him down to three."

Rob looked at Bernie and raised his eyebrows. From the disgusted look on his probation officer's face, he decided to just sit, looking as bored as he felt.

"Kid, you really should improve your sense of humor and understanding of life. The Jews get all our money at Christmas and they don't even believe in it."

The secretary and her boss both had the same intent, but she got to Marvin first. "You're out of here, right now." She grabbed him by the coat sleeve and pulled him toward the door.

Marvin let himself be led away while muttering over his shoulder, "Nothing but a bunch of scrooges in here. No holiday spirit. You'll probably end up with a lump of coal in your stocking. Well, Merry Christmas, anyway."

The probation officer sat down and looked up at the ceiling. "Don't pay any attention to Marvin. He suffers from having an I.Q. that would freeze water. Well, anyway, as I was saying, I do have a proposition for you. Yesterday, a local businessman came to the office and asked if I knew of anyone who needed a place to stay over the holidays. Let's see, his name is. . ." Bernie turned his desktop calender around and read the notation. "Saul Grossberg."

"Saul Grossberg?"

"Hm hum. He's the new manager of the Sears store that just opened a few months ago."

Rob studied his hands. "Really Bernie, I'd rather just be by myself. I'll find some place to stay."

"I know that. But for some reason, I've got a good feeling about this guy. I think it'd be worth the risk. What have you got to lose?"

"It's not what I've got to lose, it's just that I've got nothing to give." Rob tensed his jaw. "I don't want to accept charity or to put people out. They've got their own lives to live, and besides I don't belong in a person's house who runs a business after what happened last Christmas."

Bernie shrugged. "At least, would you be willing to meet him? We can walk down to his store right now if you're not too busy. He said he'd be in this morning."

Rob bit at the hangnail and finally tore it loose. Noticing the bead of blood on his thumbnail, he wiped his hand on his jeans. "I'd still just as soon not, but if that's what you want, I guess I could give it a try." He squinted at Bernie. "You've got to promise me that if things don't go well you'll get me out of this."

Nodding once, Bernie said, "You got it. Now grab your coat and let's go see what Mr. Grossberg has in mind."

The double doors leading into the Sears store were flanked by full-length display windows. On one side, a well-dressed family of mannequins, surrounded by toys, huddled around a synthetic fireplace. On the other, a pyramid of red-bowed tools, stereos, and snow blowers were no doubt intended to tempt last-minute shoppers seeking a more expensive gift. Rob and Bernie had to wend their way between knots of customers to get to the back of the store. They found the manager's office next to the customer service counter.

The door was open, and Rob saw a tall, formally dressed man talking to a saleslady. The clerk poked her finger through a hole in the side of a box while the man held the top of an electric frying pan up to the light. "Of course you can give them a full refund. It has a slight dent right here, see?" He laid the lid on the desk. "On the other hand, if they want to take it as is, give them five dollars off. Either way, let it be their choice and be sure to send them away happy."

The satisfied saleslady gathered up the box and appliance, then excused herself as she walked by. The manager saw them standing outside the doorway and gestured for them to come in. He looked first at Bernie, then quickly glanced at Rob, before extending his hand to the probation officer. "Bernie McCormick. I was hoping I would see you today." He came forward and shook his hand heartily.

Rob shifted his weight from one foot to the other

while Bernie hesitated before entering the office. "Hope we haven't caught you at your busiest time. I probably should have called for an appointment."

There was no smile on the man's face, but his eyes sparkled and his tone of voice was gentle and sincere. "That's not necessary. We should all be thankful that we are busy at this time of the year. The alternative would not be nearly as monetarily rewarding. Please come in, gentlemen."

Bernie stepped aside and motioned for Rob to precede him. "Mr. Grossberg, this is Rob Newton."

Rob offered his hand, but was embarrassed when the manager's firm grasp clasped only his extended fingers.

"I'm happy to meet you, Rob. And is Rob short for Robert?" This time his mouth turned slightly upward.

Rob cleared his throat. "No, it stands for Robin, but I don't use that name. . .anymore." He gave Bernie a pained look.

"That's too bad. Robin is a very fine name. It brings to mind images of spring and rebirth, which are so necessary to reassure us during a cold winter day like today. Nonetheless, Rob it shall be." He pointed to two chairs, then went behind his desk to the swivel chair. "Now, how can I be of service?"

Bernie broke the momentary silence. "Mr. Grossberg. . ."

The manager raised his hand, palm forward. "Please, my employees call me Mr. Grossberg. I'm Saul to my friends and would appreciate it if you, too, would call me Saul."

"Fine, I'd like that. Well Saul, yesterday you mentioned that you might be willing to have someone stay with you over the holidays. It just so happens that my friend, Rob, will not be going home this year. So I thought we might come over to discuss your generous offer."

"Good." Saul rotated his chair to face Rob. "Indeed, my wife and I would both be honored if you choose to be our guest. We can't promise a very exciting time, but there is plenty of room, our home is warm, and Irene is an excellent cook. By the way, do you ski?"

Rob wanted to say that he'd always wanted to ski, but didn't have the money, equipment, or opportunity to do so. Instead, he merely answered, "No, I guess I'm not much into sports."

"Well, if you're not an athlete, that certainly gives us something in common. The only letter I ever received was in my mother's chicken soup. But moving here has allowed me to refuel my earlier addiction to skiing. You look like a skier to me. Given the chance, I bet you'd enjoy it as much as I do. If you would allow me to introduce you to the best lifelong recreation for us non-athletes, I'd be pleased to take you up on the slopes with me tomorrow."

"Gee, I don't know. I don't have any of the stuff I'd need. Besides, don't you have to work?"

"Not really. By December twenty-fourth, business will dramatically slow down and my pre-holiday worth will be minimal. More importantly, I owe myself a day off to rejuvenate before starting inventory next week. Well, is it a deal?"

Rob shielded his eyes with his hand and tried to subtly search for an answer to his quandary on

Bernie's face. But his probation officer merely gave a noncommittal shrug of his shoulders. Rob took a deep breath, then exhaled. "Before having me in your home, don't you want to know anything about me?"

Saul made a tent with his hands and seriously considered his fingertips. "I know Bernie responded to my request and brought you here." His eyes moved to the probation officer. "I respect his judgment, since he enjoys such a fine reputation for doing his job well. Too, I know that you must have a need for a temporary safe shelter. What you don't know is that, right now, my wife and I also have a need to make our home a place where someone like you would be comfortable at this time of year."

Before Rob could respond, Saul continued, "There is something I've neglected to mention . . . about me. In our home, we don't celebrate a traditional Christmas." He waited a moment, then added, "However, I can assure you there will be no attempt to impose our religious beliefs on you. I'll take you to your own church on Christmas morning, and if you wish to honor your traditions with your own friends, we'll certainly understand. I know how strange it must seem to be invited to spend Christmastime in a Jewish home, but I certainly hope that won't negatively effect your decision to be our guest."

The word "Jewish" echoed in Rob's ears. He recalled his earlier dislike of Marvin and his distasteful joke. "If you'll have me, I'd like to take you up on your offer." He glanced over at Bernie. "I'll try not to let either of you down."

"Splendid." The manager took out his pen and

reached for the notepad in his desk. "Now, if you will tell me where to meet you, we'll get an early start tomorrow morning. Will seven-thirty be too soon?"

"No, that'll be okay. I'll be out in front of the tallest dorm on campus. But I don't have any of the right kind of equipment or ski clothes."

"That presents no problem. Just dress warmly. I have everything else you'll need. We'll have some breakfast at home before we leave."

Rob didn't sleep much that night. When he did, he dreamed of gracefully shooshing down the Alps, headed for a Swiss chalet. At six o'clock the next morning he rolled out of bed, went to the window, and pulled the curtains aside. Though it was still dark, he could tell that the blizzard had stopped and a full moon now presided over a cloudless sky. *"That's a good sign,"* he thought, *"even the weather's cooperating."*

After putting on his warmest sweater, he packed his suitcase, grabbed his bookbag, and rode the elevator to the dormitory lobby. A glimpse at his watch assured him that he was ten minutes early, so he decided to wait inside by the front doors. Sooner than he expected, he saw a pair of headlights from an approaching Jeep cut through the frosty stillness in the parking lot.

Saul Grossberg was already suited up in his color-coordinated ski outfit. He looked ready to pose for an advertisement in some vacation magazine, and provided quite a contrast to the "anything goes" ski bums Rob had watched laugh their way across the dorm lobby each weekend.

Though cordial and friendly, the Sears manager

talked little as he drove to his home on the outskirts of town. Rob noted that there was only one house on the block without Christmas lights and holiday decorations. Yet, it looked as though every light in the house had been turned on to provide a glowing welcome.

Irene Grossberg was much shorter than her husband and, without a doubt, smiled and talked more than he did. Saul's claim that his wife was "an excellent cook" proved not to be an exaggeration. The morning meal was served steaming hot, and Mrs. Grossberg insisted upon Rob eating three times as much as he normally did at the dorm.

After breakfast, they took him to an upstairs bedroom where a green and blue down-filled jacket, insulated ski pants, long johns, goggles, and wool socks were placed on the quilted spread of a four-poster bed. On the floor was a pair of blue ski boots. Rob noted that Mrs. Grossberg stood back by the doorway and seemed less happy than before.

Saul picked up the ski jacket and offered it to Rob. "Here, try this on, but I'm sure it will be the right size."

It was. Rob squeezed the padded sleeve. "How'd you know what size I wear?"

Irene came up alongside her husband and gently slapped him on the backside. "Clothes he knows. Why not, his father taught him coat sizes before he could even read. Now come on, Saul, let Robin get dressed."

Rob winced at the sound of his name. He wanted to correct the kindly lady, but thought better of it.

Just before they were ready to leave, Saul took him out to the garage and pointed to a pair of colorful laminated skis. "You'll use these today. They might be a bit short, but all the better to learn with." He then handed Rob two ski poles.

If the equipment had been used at all, it didn't show. Both the skis and poles looked brand new. Rob ran his hand from the tip of one ski down over the printed logo. He stopped as his fingers touched the engraved name near the metal bindings—Aaron Grossberg.

"Do these belong to your son?" Rob asked.

"Yes, they were my son's." Saul gently took the skis from Rob and loaded them in the rack atop the Jeep.

As they were about to drive away, Mrs. Grossberg ran from the house and signaled for Rob to roll down the car window. "Here." She slipped a soft woolen scarf around his neck and tightly tucked it into the front of his jacket. "Now, isn't that better? It'll shut out the wind and keep your neck nice and warm. I don't want you to catch a nasty cold." Then she backed away and stood in the driveway, waving as they pulled out.

A few blocks from home, Saul stopped the car and got out. "We should take off our jackets now, or we'll be chilled when we go outside." He smiled. "It saves an argument if I'm bundled up when I leave the house."

Rob unzipped the down coat. "You sure have a nice wife, Saul."

"Indeed. I've been twice blessed. To have married both a fine woman and mother is a king's treasure. Like her name implies, Irene brings a peacefulness to our home that I don't thank her for enough."

The first thirty miles of the forty-mile trip to the ski

run passed rapidly as Saul told him about edging, traversing, and righting himself across the slope before trying to get up after falling. The final winding ten miles, however, seemed to take forever as Rob watched for the ski hill to come into view around each curve in the road. When they finally did turn off the highway, he was disappointed to learn there were still seven miles of mountain road to go.

After Saul purchased the ski passes and hooked one on Rob's zipper, they clomped toward the beginner's slope. Rob was anxious to get started and give skiing his best try, but when they did reach the foot of the hill, Saul made him go through a series of stretching exercises. He wanted to tell his tutor that he was not really that out of shape, but instead followed Saul's lead in doing what seemed like squat-jumps without the jumps.

"You'll find out that skiing uses different muscles than you normally use. If more people took the time to warm up, there wouldn't be so many of them on crutches." Saul then helped him into his bindings. He made him practice falling and pushing himself up with his ski poles. He also taught him how to climb uphill, side-stepping with the edges turned in.

Rob worried that, with all the time being spent on getting ready to ski, the day would be over before he ever got on the short T-bar to attack what Saul called the Bunny Slope. After edging their way up a slight incline, Saul explained how to shift his weight from one ski to the other. Rob lost his balance and fell in slow motion like a top-heavy tree. He hit the snow-packed ground and tried to bounce back up. Forgetting his teacher's earlier lesson, he forgot to position his skis across the incline. Rob felt himself start downhill and could do nothing but painfully sit back on his skis as he rode them down the slope like a child with a new sled.

Saul came quickly to his side, and with his right ski, forced him to turn into the slope. Rob felt embarrassment mount within him, threatening to turn to anger. He probably would have lost his self-control if it weren't that while attempting to help him up, Saul too toppled over. In a few moments, both men laughed together as they lay flat on the snow.

The rest of the lesson progressed more smoothly. They again side-stepped up the slope, and this time Saul showed him snow-plow and step-turn techniques. The first trip up the T-bar was a bit more traumatic. He fell once and had to roll out of the way before oncoming skiers glided over him. On his second try, Rob managed to master the tow and now looked down from the top of the beginners' slope. This time, he tried to concentrate on Saul's words of advice as he started down the hill. Much to his surprise, he managed to snow-plow all the way down the Bunny Slope without falling and even executed one step-turn.

Saul joined him at the base and, as they remounted the tow, made a few tactful suggestions. Rob's next run turned out to be somewhat more successful than the others. The fourth and fifth times down the slope gave him added confidence. Importantly, he knew that Saul could see him doing better. During the first run after lunch, Saul urged him to put his skis closer together to better execute what he now referred to as a Stem

Christy. Before he had called it a step-turn. *"Even my vocabulary's improving,"* Rob thought as he trailed his well-coordinated teacher in wide, sweeping turns.

A glimpse at his watch confirmed that at best he would have time for two or three more runs. The ride up the T-bar no longer caused him any concern. He kept his skis in the dual ruts and even glided over a place where some beginner had left a hole after falling. Rob readied himself at the crest of the hill as Saul gracefully came to a stop beside him.

"You're probably bored stiff, having to babysit me on the Bunny Slope," Rob said.

"Not at all. You're doing really well for a novice. When we come up here the next time, I think you'll be ready for one of the lower chair lifts."

"I'd like that." Rob skidded his skis back and forth. "Really like that."

"If you'll take my advice, you should always stop once before your last run to just look around and soak up the view."

"Sounds good to me." Rob braced himself on his poles and took a deep breath of crisp winter air. Although the beginner's slope provided only a base for the towering mountain behind him, he was high enough to look down at the folded lines of skiers moving slowly toward the chair lifts. For a moment, he let his mind conjure up a feeling of being on a foreign planet where regimented clones were directed toward their assigned tasks. From his point of view, the anonymous skiers seemed much alike, with only color differentiating them. Almost all wore stocking caps with nylon ski jackets tightly zipped under their chins. All, too, peered through goggles—some grey, others yellow—in defense against the now-lowering sun.

Those riding in the double chairs which sailed overhead extended his Martian daydream. A steel tether guided the skicraft between bearing rollers on the green-painted metal towers that made a pathway to the sky.

"That's nice. Very nice." He closed his eyes and tried to lock the scene in his memory bank.

As he pushed off, Rob tried to add a bit more speed. Although he almost fell once, the turns came easier and he didn't have to closely follow Saul's downhill path. He had already turned toward the T-bar loading area when Saul joined him.

"Are you ready for your last run?" Saul asked.

Rob glanced at his watch. "Sure."

"Then it's time for the final part of your first lesson." Saul looked intently serious. "Statistics show that almost one hundred percent of the serious accidents occur during a skier's last time down the mountain. Therefore, to avoid injury, you should skip your last run." His expression remained unchanged, but his eyes showed that glint that Rob had noticed earlier.

"I guess it must be time to leave; we wouldn't want to go against the odds." Rob turned and took one last look up the hill.

Saul nodded.

Though the slight incline between the Bunny Slope and the lodge was far less steep than the one he had been skiing on, it was well packed and icy. Rob used an exaggerated snow plow as he carefully pushed off downhill.

Someone behind him screamed, "Look out below, I'm

comin' through!" There was no time to adjust before Rob was knocked to the ground in a mixmaster of flying skis and poles.

He heard Saul's voice close to his ear. "Don't move until you're sure you're okay."

"I think I'm all right, if you'll just help me get untangled." Rob felt Saul carefully sort out the skis and boost him upright.

The other man's stocking cap was pulled down over his face, but Rob recognized the voice that said, "Talk about a runaway train. You should have got out of the way when I yelled. Now, how about giving me a hand, buddy."

"Oh no. Not you again, Marvin." Rob winced as he touched the bump on the back of his head.

Instead of the asked-for help, Saul pointed his index finger at the pudgy skier. Though he didn't raise his voice, he spoke in a tone that Rob hadn't heard before. "It wasn't his responsibility to get out of your way. You're supposed to watch out for those in front of you." He jerked Marvin up. "You were completely out of control. Next time, you should sign up with the ski school before you seriously hurt someone."

"Yeah, sure." Marvin brushed some snow from his jacket. "Sorry, kid. But I gotta get going. I think I can get in a couple more runs before they shut down." He pointed his skis toward the lift line and clumsily skidded away.

Saul shook his head. "What a careless person."

"In more ways than one," Rob added.

They removed their boots before starting home, and Rob moved his feet closer to the floor heater. "I really want to thank you...for everything today. I can't remember a time when I had more fun at Christmas." He bit his lip, wishing he'd not mentioned the word "Christmas."

"Good." Saul kept his eyes on the road. "Then that makes me happy, too. You're going to be a fine skier in no time at all, Robin. Excuse me, I mean Rob."

"That's okay. It's just that my name was part of my problem. You've been really nice to me, and although you haven't asked, you should know why I'm not going home for the holidays like everyone else." He looked at the driver, but saw no emotion expressed.

"It happened last Christmas Eve when my friend and I decided to have our own celebration. We drank way too much, and that's when I did the most stupid thing I've ever done." He cleared his throat. "He said that since my name was Robin, and his name was John, like Little John, why shouldn't we rob from the rich and give to the poor. So we broke into a department store and were loading a bunch of toys in the car when the police came. I guess we set off the burglar alarm."

"Um hmm," Saul mumbled.

"My folks were really embarrassed, and I can't fault them for that, especially when it was in the town paper on Christmas Day."

Saul interrupted for the first time. "And the merchant you stole from? How did he feel?"

"That's another weird thing. He was actually sorry to press charges, but said it was company policy to prosecute. I remember him asking me what he'd done to me to make me want to steal from him."

"Yes, I know that feeling." Saul shook his head.

"Well, I guess I was luckier than John. Since this wasn't the first time he'd been in trouble, he had to do time in the county jail. I didn't even have a speeding ticket on my record, so I got eighteen months of probation and was told that if I screwed up again, I'd end up in jail with John."

Saul asked, "Why weren't you at home on your Christmas Eve?"

Rob looked out the side window. "I don't want it to sound like I'm blaming my parents. They've both been better to me . . . than they are to each other. It's just that I never really knew if things were going to be good at home or not. I suppose they've lived a pretty hard life and probably drink too much to forget. It was usually easier to not be around. Anyway, now I've got to stay straight, pay my dues, and hope that someday the people I've hurt will somehow forgive me. But I doubt if that will happen." He wiped perspiration from his brow.

Saul reached down and turned off the fan. "I sincerely hope that none of us must go through his entire life trying to live down the mistakes of the past. We all have a need for such things as forgiveness and acceptance of our willingness to try to atone for our errors. In your case, just as I'm sure that in time you will become a fine skier, likewise I have no doubt that time will heal the wounds and you will become a credit to your family."

For a time, nothing more was said as the winter stillness filled the car.

Saul finally broke the silence. "Before we get home, I should make you aware of our customs during the

Friday night meal so that you won't be surprised. Tonight starts the *Shabbot*, what you might call the Sabbath. It ends Saturday at sundown. After Irene blesses the candles, I will then bless the wine."

Rob raised his hand. "Excuse me, but . . ."

Saul tensed and said softly, "As I promised, we will do nothing to force our beliefs on you."

"I'm not worried about that. Only I can't drink alcohol, not even wine. You know, as a condition of my probation."

"Of course." Saul sat back and refocused on the road.

"And then I bless the bread. Wait until you taste Irene's braided bread. Mmm." He pressed the fingers of his right hand together and moved it in front of his face. "Then we eat. I think you'll enjoy everything except maybe the chopped liver, and even that you might like. There will be matzo ball soup, browned potatoes, and yes, Irene's pot roast—not too fancy, but I've tasted none better—and apple strudel."

"Sounds great." Rob wiped at the corner of his mouth.

Saul smiled. "And of course, we'll *schmooze*."

"*Schmooze?*" Rob screwed up his face.

"That means to talk, or better yet, maybe even have a friendly argument. Who knows? You see, we have a custom that a family should maintain a conversation during the meal. Government, business, whatever."

They drove up the driveway, got out of the Jeep, and unloaded the skis. The aroma of cooking welcomed them home, and Rob figured a blind man could have found the front door by merely following his nose.

Once inside the house, Saul stopped and lowered his eyes. "I forgot to mention that before dinner we'll have

Yahrzeit, but it won't take long." Then he took Rob by the arm and called out, "Irene, we're home."

They walked into the dining room and around the table bedecked with glistening plates, sparkling silverware, long-stemmed goblets, and linen napkins with creases that looked sharp enough to cut your finger. Two slender candles in silver holders completed the setting.

"Irene?" Saul again called out as he walked toward the kitchen door.

Rob heard a weak answer. "I'm here." In the kitchen, Irene sobbed softly as she tried to continue peeling an apple over the sink. Her sagging shoulders made her look even smaller.

Saul walked over to his wife. "What's the matter, Renie?" When she turned around, Rob could see the bloodshot eyes and teardrops still hanging on her cheeks.

"Oh, Saul." She reached in her apron pocket and took out a folded page from a newspaper. "Look what they've done to Aaron."

As Saul unfolded the article, Rob could not avoid seeing the headline: "JEWISH GRAVES VANDALIZED."

Saul laid the paper on the cabinet next to Rob, then put his arms around his wife and pressed her head to his shoulder. "There, there. Don't cry. No one can hurt our Aaron now. It's only cold marble that has been marred."

Rob looked down at the newspaper photograph and could make out the spray-painted swastikas and lightning bolts superimposed on the etched Star of David and Aaron Grossberg's name.

Saul patted his wife's head. "Would you like to rest

for awhile? Rob and I will finish preparing dinner."

"No. I'll serve. Better to keep busy." She eased herself away from her husband and wiped her eyes with the hem of her apron. "You two go sit in the living room. I'll call you in about ten minutes, when I finish the strudel."

Before they left the kitchen, Rob came forward and stood next to Mrs. Grossberg. "I'm very sorry for what's happened. It's just not right for nice people like you to be hurt, especially when you've been so kind to someone without a home at Christmastime. I wish there was something I could do."

She patted his cheek. "Thank you, Robin. It's so nice to have you here with us. Besides, I never know how to cook for only two."

Saul insisted that Rob sit in a large overstuffed chair, while he bent down to light the gas fireplace. He straightened up and took a silver-framed photograph from the mantle. "This was taken of Aaron last year. He would have been just about your age." He handed it to Rob.

The picture was taken from a sideview and the edge of a black and gold skullcap was barely visible behind the curly hair. The young man had his father's eyes and his mother's smile. Rob carefully handed it back to Saul. "Why would people do horrible things to someone's grave that they don't even know?"

Saul sighed as he centered the photograph on the mantle. "I have always been taught that man is basically good, and I suppose I still believe it. But, for some of us there is a dark side; a dimension of our character that cries out for someone—or something—to hate and feel superior to. If unchecked by law, or courage, or conscience, this need to hate and destroy can cause the horror that was Holocaust or the bigotry and bias that keeps us from living better, more peaceful lives. My people have, unfortunately, too often suffered from being the focal point of such malice. The reason? I don't honestly know. Maybe it is merely because we exist."

Rob's mind searched for something, anything to say. He felt relieved when Saul continued. "We must, however, try to live our lives in such a way as to be of use to humanity, while never forgetting the slaughter or allowing the Adolf Hitlers to ever again commit their atrocities."

Boosting himself out of the chair, Rob went to the fireplace. "I wish I could have met your son. Bernie's told me to pick my friends carefully, and it would have done me a lot of good to be around a guy like Aaron."

Saul warmed his hands. "Yes, you two would have gotten along quite well. He was sensitive like you are, and outgoing."

"I don't know how to say it the right way, but you and Mrs. Grossberg must miss him so much. Yet you take a stranger into your house."

"A stranger? Only at first. At times today, it was as if I were able to again enjoy my son's company and help him learn how to ski. I am especially thankful for this memory, since this evening, December twenty-fourth, is the anniversary of our Aaron's death."

Rob felt his jaw drop and instinctively reached up to cover his mouth. "Wow, I didn't . . . ."

"I shouldn't be making you feel our sadness. That

was not my intent when I invited you to be our guest. Do you remember when we were coming back from skiing, and I told you I hoped none of us should go through life regretting his past mistakes?"

"Uh huh."

"Well, I was really trying to reassure myself as much as you."

For the first time since returning home, the lump on Rob's head ached. He reached up and touched it with his fingers. "I guess I don't understand."

Saul turned his back to the fire and looked up at the ceiling. "In my life, I, too, have made my share of mistakes. But the worst was when I encouraged Aaron to go out and enjoy himself that evening. He was at home comfortably watching TV. Since most of the programs were about a holiday that is not of our tradition, I urged him to go to a movie with some of his friends. The streets were icy, there was an accident with another car driven by a drunken driver, and I lost my son."

Rob put his hand on Saul's shoulder. "You really can't blame yourself for what happened. You said that Aaron was comfortable. Well, I can sure see why. My parents were always after me to stay home, but I never felt at peace there. Bernie says that sometimes bad things happen to good people, when no one is to blame. I think your son must have had a wonderful life and was lucky to have the parents he did."

"I do thank you, Rob, for your kind words, but . . . ."

Irene's voice broke the tension. "It's time" echoed through the house. Saul went to a cabinet and took out a skull cap, which he called a *yarmulke*.

When Saul lit the *Yahrzeit* candle to honor the anniversary of their son's death, Rob again saw the pain etched on his hosts' faces. Then following the chanting to bless the candles, wine, and bread, a meal was served that exceeded even Saul's praise of his wife's cooking aptitude. To Rob, it was like an artist's pallet of contrasting colors and scents. Each serving tasted better than the one before, except for maybe the chopped liver, which he washed down with a drink of water. And even it wasn't all that bad.

As promised, they *schmoozed* about everything from politics to boys' hair styles. Rob found himself supporting Mrs. Grossberg more often than siding with Saul, who usually spoke to the more controversial point of view.

After dinner, his wife accepted Saul's offer to do the dishes and decided that perhaps she would rest for awhile. When the kitchen was cleaned and the silverware stored in felt-lined boxes, Saul offered to give Rob his first bridge lesson. Later, Irene joined them, and Rob found himself in the middle of contradictory suggestions made by his two teachers.

Rob was especially happy when Saul mentioned that after services tomorrow, they might be able to get in a half-day's skiing. He asked Saul if his religion allowed recreation on the Sabbath. "Of course. That's when we are to put work aside and enjoy ourselves."

When Rob went to bed, sleep didn't come easily. Even resurrecting the view from the top of the ski slope in his mind did little to calm the gnawing anxiety that kept him awake. After an hour of tossing, he got up, slipped on his Levis, picked up his bookbag, and quietly opened the bedroom door.

* * * * * * * * * *

The soft knock and Irene's invitation to breakfast prompted Rob to throw back the covers and force himself to a sitting position. It had been a short night and he probably would have slept until noon had he not been called. *"Christmas morning,"* Rob thought as he rubbed the grit from his eyes.

When Irene had cleared the dishes following another beautifully cooked meal, Saul stood up and put his arm around his wife. "Rob, we would like you to have Aaron's ski outfit and equipment." He kissed his wife on the forehead. "But you must understand, this is not a Christmas present, merely a gift to a friend."

Rob searched his mind for an appropriate way to say thanks. He was finally able to say, "You two have already done so much for me, and now this. I . . . ." He got up and, after asking to be excused from the table, mumbled, "I'll be right back," as he left the room.

He returned shortly with his sketchbook in hand. "I wish I'd had more time to do it better." Opening the cardboard cover, he carefully separated a sheet from the wire binding and handed it to Saul.

Saul looked down at the drawing, then started to say something. Instead, he merely nodded and held it so that his wife could see it better.

Irene's eyes opened to full aperture. "Why, that's us and Aaron, again together at our table. And the candles, and the bread. Oh Robin, it's so beautiful."

Saul pursed his lips, then shook Rob's hand. "This

is the picture I never got around to taking. Only it's better than a photograph, because of the feeling expressed. I can't believe you could draw our son so well, when you never even met him. We'll never be able to thank you enough."

Rob had to clear his throat before he could say anything. "I sure hope you like it. I wanted to give you something to say thanks for all you've done."

"So you gave of yourself." Saul smiled warmly. "And what a wonderful gift you have to give."

* * * * * * * * * *

Rob had almost finished telling Bernie about his Christmas weekend when he was interrupted by Marvin's voice outside the office.

"Yeah, I know he's in conference, Irm. But maybe he'll be a little more sympathetic than you are."

When Marvin appeared in the doorway on crutches, it took a maximum effort on Rob's part to keep from laughing out loud.

Straining to make the crutches work while keeping his cast off the floor, Marvin puffed his way into the office. "Kid, you better get up and let me sit down or I'm liable to fall all over you again." Rob stood up and moved the chair so that Marvin could ease his weight onto it.

"Well," Marvin said to Bernie, "aren't you going to ask?"

The probation officer seemed to also have trouble keeping a straight face. "All right. How did you manage to screw up your leg?"

Marvin set the crutches aside. "'Took a real header,

and the darn bindings didn't release. What a way to spend the Christmas holiday."

Rob tried to look as serious as possible. "And I'll bet it happened on your last run."

"That's right, kid. How'd you know that?"

Bernie leaned over his desk and whispered, "Did I forget to tell you? He's psychic. You know, sixth sense, ESP, and all that."

"No kidding?" Marvin made an effort to get up, then slumped back in the chair. "Well, I only stopped by to wish you a Happy New Year."

Bernie walked around the desk and stood next to Rob. "Yes, I think . . . no, I know it's going to be a very fine year."

Rob heard the party sounds of corks popping, and people laughing, and a band playing "Auld Lang Syne," echoing deep within himself.

Christmas Alchemy

As Eileen Donahue watched the ditto machine rhythmically crank out the Christmas programs, she once again reflected on how much she enjoyed being secretary of Lincoln School. She could not imagine another occupation that would afford her more happy, peaceful moments, except for those few occasions when an eruption occurred in the adjoining principal's office and the air was rent by an outburst that seemed so ill-placed in an elementary school.

She especially appreciated having a work schedule that so closely approximated her own children's school hours and allowed her holidays during the same days they were home. She felt gratified that she had a function in the education of children and took pride in serving teachers so they could be free to spend more time teaching students.

Eileen smiled as she became aware that the Christmas carol being enthusiastically sung by Miss Silver's fourth grade class across the hall was in sync with the clicking, whirring duplicating machine. After looking around to gain assurance that she was still alone in the outer office and that the principal could not see her, she allowed herself the privilege of moving her hand in time with the singing—musically directing the clearly printed, pink papers onto their assigned stacks.

She noted that there were but a few remaining sheets left to be fed into the machine and felt a minor irritation at having to shut off the duplicator before the children finished "decking the halls with boughs of holly." Nonetheless, with the ditto machine turned off, the final "fa la la la laaaa, la la la la" came through sure and true. She heard Miss Silver tell her class that they had done an extraordinarily fine job. "Even the Welsh people who gave us this beautiful carol would be proud to have you singing their song."

As the secretary refilled the duplicator with a healthy gulp of liquid and added a fresh pile of pink paper to the intake tray, she again marveled at Miss Silver's ability to say just the right things to make children, a secretary, fellow teachers, or even her principal feel that each one's effort is appreciated. The whole school was as pleased as she was when it became known that the elderly yet beautiful, silver-haired Miss Silver would be getting married during Christmas vacation. The fact that her husband-to-be bore the name of Mr. Gold, added an element to the children's already overflowing holiday excitement that had the entire school aglow.

The sound of the telephone receiver being slammed into its cradle in the principal's office, followed by a interconnected string of mutterings being forcibly emitted, completed destroyed her reverie. Shaking her head, she picked up the pink programs and hurriedly went to close the outer hallway door.

She read somewhere that Mark Twain felt that one needed both the "words and the music" in order to swear proficiently. Without doubt, her principal, Mr. Michael O'Day, had at his grasp both of the necessary prerequisites. She thought it a paradox that he was normally so caring, considerate, and calm under stress, and yet at other times he seemed to vent his anger by swearing. His behavior patterns had been well established during other outbursts, and Eileen knew that, as soon as he seethed for a few moments, then regained some degree of control, her boss would soon be coming out of his office to explain his latest frustration. She decided to forego stapling the programs in order to take refuge behind her desk. It was undoubtedly time to work on the attendance report.

As expected, Mr. O'Day soon sat in the chair in front of her desk. However, one quick glance told her that this time might be different. His face was reddened, and the letter in his outstretched, trembling hand was crackling as it responded to the shaking it was receiving.

Instead of anger, the secretary sensed a tone of despair in Mr. O'Day's voice. "Just look at this, Eileen." He tossed the paper toward her.

She picked up the letter and recognized it as a standard "Leave Request Form—Certificated Personnel." The form had been fastidiously completed in Miss Silver's distinctively recognizable handwriting. Her request for a personal leave day had been appropriately checked and the "Explanation-Section" had noted that she was requesting "to be absent on

December 22, the last day of school before the Christmas vacation, to be married." She added that she and Mr. Gold "were planning to fly to Hawaii for their honeymoon and the only available flight left early the morning of the twenty-third." She gave assurance that she would be especially careful to make appropriate provisions and plans for the substitute.

The teacher concluded her narrative by apologizing for having to request an absence, yet thanking the school district and administrators for their consideration.

The Leave Request Form was signed by Miss Silver and under, "Approval Routing," Mr. O'Day had added his consent with his almost indecipherable signature.

She now knew the reason for the principal's latest outburst and the resultant look of despair etched on his down-turned face. Someone had taken a red pen and scratched through the checked block requesting personal leave and had dramatically marked the square preceding the statement "Extends a Holiday." Another category, listed at a lower level on the form, was also checked in red: "Absence from school without pay may be applied for, but is not automatically granted." Miss Silver's narrative explanation was followed by the crimson script, "Denied, see policy 7.1C in Master Agreement." The endorsement section following the title, "Personnel Director," was signed, Dr. George R. Brewer (e. h.).

Eileen shook her head and sensed the principal was waiting for her to respond. "Is there a chance that this is all a misunderstanding? Look, Dr. Brewer didn't even sign the form. The 'e. h.' stands for Ellen Hanson, his secretary."

"No way. That mental midget knows exactly what's going on. He just didn't have the guts to sign it himself. He's not even in his office this morning. Doing research, his secretary says. Delegate and disappear. He's made a whole career of vanishing when he has to be responsible for his cruddy decisions."

The principal took the form from Mrs. Donahue and started pacing back and forth in front of her desk. "In thirty-four years of teaching in this school district, you know how many days of Personal and Business Leave Irene Silver has taken? Zip! Not even one day. When she turned in this form a couple of weeks ago, I looked it up. Sick leave in thirty-four years—five days. That's when she caught the chicken pox from the kids during her first year. Doggone it, if administrators can't make decisions based on common sense judgments, why don't they replace us with the cheapest computer Radio Shack puts out?"

Eileen could feel the anger welling in her administrator. "What's the policy that's referred to? Is there such a thing?" she asked.

"Sure, there's a stupid regulation." Michael O'Day went into his office and returned with an orange pamphlet titled *Agreement Between the Board of Trustees of School District No. 1 and the Elmwood Education Association.*

"It's right here on page 14." The principal opened the booklet and slapped it down in front of the secretary. In a sarcastic tone he read aloud, "The personal/business days should not be used the day(s) immediately preceding or following any scheduled holiday(s), the first two or the last two days of school."

Eileen stared down at the pamphlet and attempted to reread the policy.

"I knew it was there, but I figured there must be some discretion that could, no—must—be used. I thought maybe this could be interpreted as an emergency." His shoulders drooped, and he took a deep breath. "I don't know what I thought except that, of all the teachers in this world, Miss Silver deserves all the consideration we can give her. Makes you ashamed to be part of our great administrative team. We're nothing but a bunch of nonfeeling, uncaring misfits trying to get our jelly beans by establishing power bases within our little kingdoms."

"Would it do any good to call the superintendent?" Eileen asked in a less than optimistic tone of voice.

"You know the answer to that. I suppose he was a good administrator at one time, but he's been hit on the head so often, he's just trying to hold on until retirement. He told me last year that he's bought his gravestone here in Elmwood and will do whatever he has to do, to be buried under it. Besides that, Brewer has been undercutting him whenever possible and has the school board coming to him for most of the answers the superintendent should be giving."

The principal picked up the school policy booklet and took it back into his office. Returning, he walked past the secretary without looking at her. "Going down to the boilerroom." He then stopped and added, "Eileen, remind me to see Miss Silver this afternoon. I don't want to bother her while she's teaching. Besides, I don't know what I'm going to say, anyway."

The principal opened the hallway door, and the secretary could see the children lining up to go outside for recess. As usual, Miss Silver was as bundled up as they were. Even though there was a playground aide, the teacher always went outside with the children during recess. "It gives me the chance to walk with the boys and girls and share their thoughts outside the structured classroom," she told Eileen once when the secretary asked her why she was the only teacher to accompany her students outside during the morning reprieve.

Her principal absented himself from the office for most of the morning, and once Eileen looked out of the office window and saw him apparently taking a solitary walk around the building. The day was overcast, and the chilling breeze would make one wonder about the judgment of a jacketless man slowly shuffling over the snowpacked sidewalks with his chin down and hands thrust deeply in his pockets.

The rest of the day passed rapidly, as Eileen's school life was saturated to overflowing with the normal pre-holiday ado. She finished duplicating the musical programs, took care of her regular secretarial tasks connected with teachers' registers and lunch count, then appreciatively accepted the proudly presented student-made Christmas cards addressed to herself and Mr. O'Day.

Only one disciplinary situation was referred to the principal's office, and luckily it involved one of Miss Silver's pupils. Bill Jull had punched a sixth grader for "picking on" one of the students in his fourth grade class. It was amazing how less often Billy was sent to the office since he had been placed in Miss Silver's charge. His father was well known throughout Elmwood due to the many times his name appeared in the Police Court section of the newspaper. She had heard that he was chronically unemployed and even failed to attend the parent-teacher conference when Billy was retained in the first grade.

Miss Silver arrived in the principal's office only seconds after the playground aide hauled in the two boys. After ascertaining that there was no damage to anything but the sixth grader's ego, she sent the older student to his room and informed the secretary that this incident represented only "a temporary regression on William's part. One that would not be repeated in the future since he is one of my most dependable citizens."

Mr. O'Day's inner office door was closed most of the afternoon although there were a few grumblings due to his inability to make telephone connections with Mr. Brewer. Eileen sensed that the additional telephone calls had not changed the unpleasant administrative duty that her principal would soon be forced to face. The dismissal bell released a torrent of excited youngsters into the hallways, and Mrs. Donahue was greeted by a chorus of Merry Christmases extended to her from youngsters who passed the office door. The building cleared, besting even the record time established during the most well-organized fire drill.

As quietness filled the evacuated hallways, Eileen looked toward the inner office and wondered if it would help to give a perfunctory reminder to Mr. O'Day about his need to see Miss Silver. It became unnecessary, since the silver-haired teacher now entered the office accompanied by a slender, softly smiling student.

"Mrs. Donahue," Miss Silver started, "of course, you know Lenore Grossclose, my poetess."

Eileen returned the girl's smile. "Yes, I certainly do know Lenny."

"Well, Lenore has generously designed a Christmas greeting card for you and Mr. O'Day. The class voted to adopt it as their combined gift to both of you, in appreciation for the many services you and he have provided to make Lincoln School such a fine educational institution. Would you see if Mr. O'Day is free so that she can present it to you?"

Since the principal's door was closed, the secretary pressed the intercom button and spoke into the plastic unit. "Mr. O'Day? Miss Silver and a student are here to see you. Can you come out now?"

"All right." There was a short pause, "I'll be right there."

The principal emerged from the inner office and, although noticeably less then enthusiastic, did manage a weak smile for his audience. Miss Silver stepped back leaving the young girl center stage to make her presentation. Lenore handed the homemade envelope to the secretary and added, "This Christmas message comes from all the students in Miss Silver's fourth grade."

The enclosed card was made of blue construction paper, tastefully decorated with a stenciled silhouette of the nativity scene carefully sprayed on its front cover. Eileen opened the folded art piece and read the simple five-line message:

Celebration
Christ's birth...
Service to mankind
A message to all
Christmas.

"How beautiful, Lenny. Just look at this, Mr. O'Day." She handed the folded card to her principal. He accepted it and carefully examined the silhouette. He then held it at arm's length and squinted at it while nodding his head.

"That's really good art work. Just the right colors, too. Did you do this all by yourself, Lenny?"

"No, sir. Two other girls and I did the design. Some of the boys sprayed it for us. It's really more of a class project."

"Well, it is really nice." He then opened the card and moved his mouth as he silently read the verse.

"It's a cinquain," the young girl added. "Miss Silver has been helping me learn about other poetic forms."

Again, the principal nodded, "Beautifully done."

Eileen added, "I can see why Miss Silver calls you her poet, I mean poetess."

Miss Silver stepped beside her student and beamed proudly as she placed her arm around the girl's lean shoulders in order to give her a reassuring hug.

"Well, now we must be going. Thank you both for so graciously accepting our Christmas message." The silver-haired teacher turned to leave.

The principal cleared his throat. "Uh, Miss Silver,

when you have a moment, could I please see you . . . in your room?"

"Certainly, Mr. O'Day. I believe Lenore must be hurrying home now, but my room is in complete disarray. Could we talk here?"

Lenny wished all a Merry Christmas and, after receiving Miss Silver's dismissing nod, hurriedly left the office.

Mr. O'Day stood by his office door and held out his hand in an inviting gesture that offered the older teacher a chair beside his desk.

The inner office door remained open and Eileen wondered whether she should leave or remain at her desk. She decided that it would be best to stay so that she could answer phone calls or take care of any business that might be brought to the office. She did, however, go over once again to close the hallway door.

From her position behind her desk, she could see Miss Silver but not her principal.

The teacher spoke first, "Now, I suppose that you are about to warn me about the religious content of Lenore's poem. But, since it was her inner thoughts and personal gift to give. . . ."

The principal's voice was extremely subdued and the secretary suffered with him as he informed Miss Silver that it was not due to the Christmas card, but another matter that prompted their conference. He noted that he often hated some of the "lousier, hurtful aspects of my job." She then saw Miss Silver take the negated Leave Request Form from the principal's outstretched hand.

Eileen watched the wrinkles appear on the teacher's

brow while the starch seemed to wilt from Miss Silver's straight-backed posture. It took two readings before the elderly teacher handed the form back to the principal. Eileen reached for a Kleenex in her top drawer and looked away so as not to be seen sniffling or see the tears that were most certainly concurrently forming in Miss Silver's eyes.

Moments passed with nothing said. Then she heard Mr. O'Day start, "Irene, for the first time in my life, I don't know what to say. But. . .anyway, of course this changes nothing. . .much. You're still going to be gone. I've never told anyone this before, but why not just be sick?"

More silence.

"Or I'll take your class, or the school system can keep their money and you just go on and enjoy your wedding as much as possible. You probably weren't even aware of this idiotic policy."

Miss Silver tried to remove a restriction in her throat. The words came out slowly but clearly enunciated. "Mr. O'Day, first let me say that I fully understand that this is not a pleasant task for you to perform and that I bear you no malice nor hold you at fault. I would, however, be less than honest if I didn't admit to my disappointment. Nonetheless, I was, and am, fully aware of the school district's policies. Mr. Gold and I read the particular section referred to in Mr. Brewer's comments very carefully before submitting my request.

"I believe the words used in the policy are *should not*. Personal leave *should not* be used on days immediately preceding a school holiday. Perhaps, as my students do, I added my meaning to the policy based on my personal field of experience. I assumed that *should not* was advisory rather than the more restrictive terms *cannot* or *will not.* I supposed that exceptions to the advice would be determined in consideration of the employee's past performance or the record of personal leave days used."

She reached for her throat and held it as she swallowed. "We also felt that the intent of the policy was to discourage personal desires to extend a holiday. As Mr. Brewer must be well aware, the imposed scheduled time of our flight affected my decision to ask for permission to leave school early. Although it will only be a small family wedding, we thought it best to have the ceremony on Friday morning so we would have time for last minute trip preparations." The elderly teacher emitted a heavy sigh and looked up at the ceiling.

"Irene," the principal said, then repeated, "Irene...."

"Excuse me, Mr. O'Day," Miss Silver continued. "I believe I've regained my composure now. Mr. Gold and I will reschedule our wedding to a later afternoon hour Friday after school. And I shall most assuredly be at my teaching station as encouraged by the school policy. While I do appreciate your willingness to provide for my personal needs, I could not, nor would I, place you in the compromising position of being a party to my violating the sick leave provision or officially attesting to my presence when, indeed, I was absent from school."

"Irene...."

"And lastly, Mr. O'Day, I wish to put this matter entirely at rest following our conference. I don't want you feeling badly about this situation, which is well beyond your control. My life, as well as my teaching position, has been rich indeed, and I learned long ago to put minor problems such as this into proper perspective. Now, I really must ask to be excused as Mr. Gold and I have some details to rearrange. And, yes, Michael, thank you so much for the caring concern you've exhibited."

As the teacher walked through the outer office and bid Eileen a "good evening," the secretary noted that beautiful Miss Silver was once again in charge and that her backbone had received a renewed supply of starch.

Mrs. Donahue waited for a moment, then went to the principal's doorway. "Is everything all right?" she asked.

"Yes, I'm okay. Not a very good feeling, but all right. Did you hear that? She called me Michael. That's a first. Michael. Wow."

As the final week of school sped by, Eileen sensed that the story of Miss Silver's leave request being denied had occupied most of the talking time in the teacher's lounge and had been the daily table topic in the staff lunch room. On one occasion, when she went to fill her coffee cup, conversation between staff members abruptly stopped as she entered the room. *I hope they don't blame me,"* she thought, as she returned to her desk within the sanctuary of the principal's office.

On the next to last day of school, a three-member delegation of students from Miss Silver's room came to the office and asked to see the principal. Sharon Pitrowski explained that she, as class president, Lenny Grossclose, the class secretary, and Billy Jull, sergeant at arms, had been delegated by their class club to express their "deep-felt feelings" to the school principal, as well as to make certain requests.

Mr. O'Day met with them in the outer office and invited them to sit around the conference table.

Although used to leading cheers at school functions, Sharon Pitrowski had trouble beginning the discussion, but after receiving a motivating nudge from Billy Jull, she introduced the topic. She pointed out that this visit had been the class's idea and that Miss Silver had only consented to allow them to go after their teacher was reminded that she had continually encouraged them "to at all times speak your minds to the proper authority when you observe an injustice." Sharon noted how disturbed the class was to hear that Miss Silver had to rearrange her wedding. Each sentence in the student's grievance was punctuated by Billy's muttered exclamation, "What a rip-off."

Lenny had come equipped with a secretarial notepad and from the beginning of the meeting took copious notes. At one point, Billy seemed to be firing up with his "rip-off" remarks and Lenny calmly placed a hand on his shoulder to subdue his zeal.

It now became time for the principal's rejoinder. He assumed a very serious demeanor. "Kids, you should know that I'm no happier about the situation than you are. You'll learn later on in life that sometimes you have to go along with, or even enforce, rules you don't believe in."

Billy interrupted, "What did you do to change 'em?"

"What was that, Billy?" the principal asked.

"In our club meetings, Miss Silver taught us that if we were put in a position to have to go by bad rules, it was our duty to work to get 'em changed. What did you do to change 'em?"

Mr. O'Day's eyes opened wider as he sat erect. Billy looked directly at him, hands braced on the table, ready for fight or flight. The principal eased back in his chair and scratched his chin.

"Well, Billy, not enough, that's for sure. As usual, Miss Silver's point is well taken, and I agree that I should have previously put forth effort toward improving the policy."

"What a rip-off."

Eileen saw the class president becoming more and more nervous. Lenny busied herself by writing faster than ever.

"Well, if there's nothing that can be done...," Sharon started to say.

Again Billy interrupted, "You know, this school should really treat Miss Silver best of all. Do you realize what a rotten kid I was and how many times I got sent to this office before I got put in her room? We're keeping a chart on how many times I get in trouble, and I've gone way down. What a rip-off."

Mr. O'Day reassured the students that he felt that Miss Silver was especially worthy of their praise.

Sharon squirmed in her chair. "Well, then that's that. Thank you, Mr. O'Day, for listening to us." She stood up and motioned with her head toward the door.

Lenny whispered to her, "The party. You forgot to mention the party."

"Right," Sharon said while still backing slowly toward the door. The words came rapidly. "Tomorrow afternoon we want to have a wedding party, a shower, I think they call it, for Miss Silver and Mr. Gold at two o'clock. Okay? And yes, although some kids weren't too happy with it, you and Mrs. Donahue are invited. Okay? But, Mrs. Donahue, I didn't mean the kids are mad at you. Okay? Well then, that's that. Meeting adjourned."

The students started to leave, but Mr. O'Day beat them to the door, assured them that the party was a fine idea, thanked them for coming to see him, and shook their hands as they left the office.

The weather refused to change, even if it was December twenty-second and the last day of school before a holiday break. It was gray and overcast when Eileen arrived at work and she wondered if the cold, dreary day would dampen the children's excitement in anticipation of the long-awaited Christmas vacation. As the children swarmed into the building, their faces radiated elements of warmth and sunlight that seemed to take the chill off Lincoln Elementary School. Members of Miss Silver's fourth grade class seemed far less subdued than normal, and the room across the hall was alive with holiday merriment.

The tardy bell created its usual quieting effect on the building and the secretary settled into her morning routine. She didn't see her principal much, as he was, no doubt, arranging the gymnasium to accommodate the entire school during the mid-morning program.

Even the afternoon session started as usual, except that a few hundred children had made it a point to stop by the office to wish her and Mr. O'Day a "Merry Christmas." Then the superintendent arrived at the building and took the principal with him while he performed his annual perfunctory duty of rapidly going to each room and wishing the teacher and children "joy and well-being during the mid-winter holiday season."

She nervously waited for the principal to return from his tour of the building in order to be on time for Miss Silver's party, since the invitation had clearly stated that the shower would begin promptly at two o'clock. Mr. O'Day and the superintendent entered the office at five minutes after two and went directly to the inner office behind a closed door.

She could not avoid hearing the one-way conversation being delivered by her principal and told herself that she didn't really hear Mr. O'Day saying that ". . . the educational world would be much better if they pinched the heads off power-hungry little men like our beloved personnel director." Eileen felt she had to avoid further criticism of her boss, from Miss Silver's students, for missing the party. She pressed the intercom button and as tactfully as possible apologized for interrupting, but felt that Mr. O'Day would not want to be any later than he already was in arriving at Miss Silver's party.

The inner office door burst open and her principal grabbed her by the arm, moving her toward the classroom across the hall. He spoke over his shoulder to his superintendent, "Next year, I'm going to personally try to get that policy changed so that this doesn't ever happen again."

As they entered the fourth grade room, some of the children started clapping, but the secretary could not help but see and feel the reproachful glare fixed upon them by Billy Jull. She also saw him silently mouthing "What a rip-off." He then turned his attention back to the opening of presents portion of the shower.

Although she hadn't seen the elderly gentleman standing beside Miss Silver enter the building, she knew that indeed this must be Mr. Gold. It struck her as almost mystic that he looked so much like Miss Silver. He exuded the same warmth, the same silent strength of conviction. Yes, and like her, his eyes twinkled when he smiled, clearly demonstrating a retained element of youth. In one matter, they definitely differed. While the teacher's neatly sculpted locks seemed to provide a backdrop for her perpetually smiling face, his receding hairline left but single strands, which were judiciously combed forward in an attempt to camouflage his baldness. Also, in contrast to Miss Silver, his remaining hair still kept a tinge of golden hue.

The presents were displayed on a book table in the front of the room. Even though she had already received at least five other bottles of bubble bath, Miss Silver carefully unwrapped Sharon's box of *Pearls of Joy Bubble Bath.* It was appreciatively received and proudly displayed to Mr. Gold. When he said, "What a lovely gift from such a beautiful young lady," the class president and cheerleader blushed, then happily skipped back to her desk.

The table was also well stocked with a complete assortment of soap. *"Maybe the children took the word shower literally,"* Eileen thought as Billy Jull took his present forward to his favorite teacher. There was no doubt that the youngster had wrapped the package himself. Apparently there was no scotch tape at his house, but the masking tape had at least served the purpose of holding last year's Christmas paper around the present.

"My, but this is a heavy one, William," Miss Silver remarked as her fingers lifted the tape up by the edges so as not to tear the colorful wrap.

Tears that had been skillfully held back for much of that afternoon now filled the teacher's eyes as she proudly displayed a bound copy of the *Coronet Everyday Encyclopedia—Volume 1, A-B.* Mrs. Donahue recognized the text as one selling for forty-nine cents at the local supermarket. Mr. Gold moved closer to his wife-to-be and gently put his arm around her waist.

"I know how much you like to read," Billy said, "and I bet he likes to read, too. So I thought a book would be just the thing for your honeymoon in Hawaii."

Instead of the anticipated well-phrased remarks that had followed the previous gift-giving, Miss Silver merely said, "Thank you, William. You'll never know how much we'll treasure this present." She then bent over and kissed the boy on the forehead.

"Aw, Miss Silver," Billy groaned, but his face showed only pride as he returned to his desk.

Since no other gifts remained to be opened, Eileen

sensed that Miss Silver was gathering her thoughts once again to express her appreciation to the modern-day Magi.

Sharon Pitrowski raised her hand. "Miss Silver. Miss Silver. There's one more, Miss Silver. You haven't got Lenny's yet."

The teacher smiled at the slender girl in the back of the room and held out her hand in a gesture of encouragement to come forward.

Suddenly the room became still, with knowing glances being given from one student to another, as Lenore Grossclose worked her way forward.

As she handed the rolled-up scroll to the grey-haired teacher, she added, "I'm sorry, Miss Silver, that I didn't have this ready to be placed on your gift table. I didn't finish it until after lunch."

Miss Silver removed the ribbon that held the rolled-up paper. She motioned for Mr. Gold to stand beside her so they could view the contents together. Her eyes moved across the page, and this time there was no effort to hold back the tears. Mr. Gold removed a handkerchief from his jacket pocket and handed it to his future wife.

"You read it, Lenny." Billy Jull quietly commanded.

"We want to hear your poem," someone in the back of the room said. Then other pleas from throughout the class were added.

Lenore looked at Miss Silver through her own water-filled eyes, then out at the class. "I don't think I can, Mrs. Donahue, would you please do it?"

It took a while for the request to break through the secretary's emotion-packed thoughts. Before she could respond, a chorus of voices were calling out to her and Billy Jull was ushering her toward the front of the room.

"I don't know if I can do it either, Lenny," the secretary said. "But I guess I'll try."

Miss Silver handed Eileen the unrolled parchment-like paper. Eileen swallowed hard and started reading:

ALCHEMY

Caringly Written by Lenore I. Grossclose

Sorcerers, and scientists too, have searched
Since days of yore
For the keys that convert a base metal
Into an expensive ore.
The solution promised riches that would
Turn beggars into kings,
Countless crowns could be cast, as well as
necklaces and rings.
Perhaps they had erred and failed to see
Their one basic flaw,
Since their vision was clouded and self-gain
Was all they saw.
Yet today, two rare substances will be
Joined into one—
Each has its qualities, no doubt the good
They've done.
And age isn't critical, they're neither
Too young nor old,
For it's only love that matters,
When Silver turns to Gold.

The class applauded loudly after Eileen finished.

Before Miss Silver was able to respond to Lenny's special gift, the wedding cake and Kool Aid were brought in. Mr. O'Day walked around the room to compliment each student while the refreshments were politely served and energetically consumed.

Sharon and two other girls asked and received permission to leave the classroom. Billy Jull left with them. Lenore organized a receiving line and had Mrs. Donahue and Mr. O'Day join the nuptial couple. Each of the class members shook their hands and then went out of the room. Miss Silver and Mr. Gold stood hand-in-hand, again thanking each student as they passed.

There were still fifteen minutes remaining in the school day when the last student passed through the receiving line and left the classroom. Eileen observed that the Christmas decorations still remained to be taken down. *"Oh well, that's something I can do,"* she thought.

Mr. O'Day had just turned to wish the couple well, when the still of the classroom was severed by the strident wailing of the Lincoln School fire alarm.

Sharon and her two friends, fully attired in their homemade cheerleading uniforms, came running in. "Now don't worry, Mr. O'Day, there's not really a fire. The bell is only a signal. Okay? Come on, Miss Silver. You too, Mr. Gold. Get your things on." The boys entered the room with boxes and started loading the wedding gifts. The cheerleaders held the elderly couple's coats and were stretching to direct the right arms into the proper sleeves.

Sharon came toward the principal. "You come, too, Mr. O'Day and Mrs. Donahue. Sorry I couldn't tell you about this. I wanted to, but the other teachers said they'd take the blame."

The wedding party was directed toward the school exit. Outside, Eileen saw that the entire student body and staff, well armed with rice, had formed a flanked pathway queuing across the playground.

As the elderly couple made their way through the rice shower, Eileen noted that the sun had broken through the cloud cover and was sending a warming beam down on the wildly cheering well-wishers.

Billy Jull held Mr. Gold's car door open. Just before she entered the passenger side, Miss Silver turned and blew a kiss toward the crowd as she gave a cheery Merry Christmas greeting. The sun seemed to be shining directly down upon her.

"Did you see that, or am I just imagining it?" the secretary said to her principal.

"No Eileen, I think I saw it, too."

Eileen's eyes were at full aperture as the golden tint reflected from the bride's previously silvered hair.

"Alchemy, indeed," she said aloud.

About the Author

Soft Sculpture by Judy Meagher
Photo by Bruce Pitcher

By his own admission, Jerry Sullivan didn't get far in life. He was born in Helena, Montana, and now is a Professor Emeritus at Montana State University—ninety miles east in Bozeman.

He claims to have written his share of arid articles for professional journals during the quarter of a century he taught in higher education. He also authored a nationally published series of textbooks optimistically intended to increase junior high school students' vocabulary.

Now in the early stages of senility, he has started his own small press, "SHAMROCK IN THE SKY BOOKS," in order to write the stories about kids, teachers, schools, and holidays that have been rattling around in his head, waiting to be told. His thirteen years as an elementary and junior high school teacher/principal have provided the admixture of memories necessary to "spin a yarn or two."

He considers storytelling to be both a privilege and a responsibility for those of Irish descent. Too, he feels that it is through our stories (or dreams) that we are able to make some sense out of this seemingly disarranged world in which we temporarily abide.

About the Illustrator

Mark Sullivan grew up illustrating textbooks and stories for his father and remembers those times as wonderful, shared experiences. A native of Montana, he draws upon a background in art, music, drama, and dance.

After attaining degrees in art and music, he embarked on a teaching career that would take him from the Fort Peck Indian Reservation to the Laboratory School of the University of Northern Colorado. Mark has recently returned to school, this time as a student again. He is currently enrolled in the Master of Fine Arts degree program in painting at Washington University in St. Louis, Missouri. Accompanying him in his current venture are his wife, Suzan, his daughter, Brianna, and his son, Conor.

As a painter involved in contemporary realism, he has always maintained a steady output of illustrations and portraits in a variety of media. His paintings and drawings continue a lifelong love affair with the portrayal of people and their conditions.

Books by Gerald D. Sullivan

Other Yuletide Yarns Series
  To Be Wanted At Christmastime—1991
  The Sound of Christmastime—1992

Tales Told Out of School Series
  Anything New in Your Life, Teach?—1991
  Grandpa's Extra Special Birthday Present—1992